I0817773

PROPENSITY

PROPENSITY

RIDLEY PARK

First published by Amazon KDP.
This Microglyphics Edition issued 2025.
Text of the work remains unchanged from the original publication.

ISBN 978-0-9710869-8-2 (Cloth Microglyphics Edition)
Also available in paperback: ISBN 979-8-2848-3868-6

Behavioural autonomy is a fragile illusion.

Disclaimer

This is a work of fiction.

Any resemblance to actual persons, living or dead, is either purely coincidental, algorithmically inevitable, or the result of ill-advised neurochemical modulation.

The events, institutions, devices, and moral frameworks depicted herein are entirely fictional. Any parallels to real-world governments, corporations, military protocols, or behaviour-manipulation initiatives are a matter for your therapist.

No Gormies were harmed in the making of this book.

Reader discretion is advised. Free will has been deprecated.

https://RidleyPark.blog

Published by Microglyphics, Cambridge, Massachusetts
Printed in the country of distribution

Dedication

This work owes its tone, its pacing, and its better instincts to the writers I've read, re-read, and quietly borrowed from – stylistically, thematically, or by way of osmosis.

To Kazuo Ishiguro, for showing how silence can speak, and how characters can unravel without anyone raising their voice.

To Cormac McCarthy, for his unpunctuated fatalism and his reverence for the void.

To Don DeLillo, for the antiseptic poetry of institutional dread.

To Margaret Atwood, for the machinery of dystopia made quietly personal.

To J.G. Ballard, for architectural horror and post-human calm.

To George Saunders, for bureaucratic absurdity rendered with surgical precision.

To Thomas Ligotti, for reminding me that existential horror can whisper.

To Emil Cioran and David Benatar, whose philosophical pessimism helped calibrate the moral compass of this book to something resembling magnetic nihilism.

And to Stanisław Lem, who proved long ago that artificial intelligence doesn't need to be sentient to unsettle us.

If this novel bears traces of their fingerprints, that is both an accident and a quiet form of gratitude.

Table of Contents

ENTROPIC 155

IMPLEMENTATION

1 · Calibration

Consciousness is the parent of all horrors.
— Thomas Ligotti

Flesh slaps steel.

One baboon hurls itself against the gate, shrieking, the sound raw and metallic, reverberating off sterile walls. Foam clings to its canines. The other responds with equal fury, claws raking the floor, tail lashing in blind rage. Between them, the transparent barrier holds, vibrating with each impact but refusing to break.

Their eyes, bloodshot. Their breath comes in bursts. Every inch: muscle, tension, intent.

If the gate drops, they would not posture. They would not hesitate. They would kill.

Behind a reinforced pane of ballistic glass – polished, smudge-free, humming faintly with air recirculation – Dr V watches with the stillness of a statue. Only his pupils move, tracking the snarls, the slams, the spectacle of fury contained by architecture.

'They've been at it for an hour,' says Dr Noor Kaplan, arms crossed, voice hollow with caution. 'If that barrier opens now, one of them doesn't leave.'

Dr V's gaze doesn't blink.

'It's gone past dominance,' he murmurs. 'This is righteousness. Ritual.

They're locked in conviction.'

Kaplan tilts her head. 'They're baboons, doctor. They don't have convictions.'

His lips move toward a smile but stop short. 'Then what we're about to give them is a mercy.'

He raises a finger.

At the console, the technician hesitates. Then presses the button.

A low-frequency tone pulses through the enclosure – too soft to register as sound, but deep enough to thrum in bone and breath, like standing beside a distant turbine. Simultaneously, the barrier begins to descend.

The instant the window touches the ground, the baboons freeze.

No sound. No motion. Just the shallow rise and fall of two torsos twitching in chemical confusion.

One tilts its head. The other blinks. No growl. No lunge.

They step forward slowly, uncertainly – two shadows closing a void. Then one extends a hand. Gently, it plucks at the other's fur, searching for nothing in particular. Grooming.

The room behind the glass exhales all at once.

Kaplan's voice comes low: 'Jesus Christ.'

Dr V says nothing at first. He's transfixed.

'It's peace,' he whispers at last. 'Synthetic, yes. But peace nonetheless.'

Kaplan doesn't take her eyes off the animals. 'You know what this reminds me of?'

He glances at her. She doesn't look away from the glass.

'The silence before a species disappears.'

The baboons continue their pantomime of affection. One nibbles gently at the other's shoulder.

Kaplan's voice softens, almost speculative. 'Imagine if we could control the world with this...'

The Doctor doesn't answer. But something behind his eyes shifts – less revelation than recognition.

Dr V's silence isn't refusal.

It's agreement.

The glass clears to a dim reflection – just Dr V's face now, superimposed over the image of two baboons grooming like monks in a trance. He stays long after the others had filed out. Kaplan offers a glance, half concern, half resignation.

She opens her mouth, then closes it.

Not the time.

The animals, once frenzied with violence, now moved with a mechanical gentleness – as if remembering a ritual they never learned. One paws lazily at the other's arm. The noise, the violence, the urgency – it's all gone. In its place: a fragile choreography of gentleness.

Dr V places his palm flat against the glass. A gesture without audience. Without purpose, even. Just the need to feel something real between him and the thing they'd made. The warmth of the barrier doesn't surprise him. The enclosure, like everything else in this facility, was calibrated – temperate, sterile, and indifferent to miracles.

This is what peace looks like, he thinks. Engineered peace. Not chosen. Not earned. Just... implemented.

He pulls his hand away and turns toward the corridor. He knows what comes next.

2 · Oversight

Man starts over again every day, in spite of all he knows, against all he knows.

— Emil Cioran

The conference room reeks of sealed air and synthetic coffee – bitter, cloying, absorbed into the carpet like institutional fatigue. Two flags stand in the corners – non-national, abstract banners in red and black, their fabric unnaturally stiff, as if starched to hold their meaningless shapes, gesturing at power without admitting provenance. On the far wall, a screen plays muted footage of the baboons' encounter on loop.

Three men are sat at the table. No insignia. No names. But their bearing is unmistakable – uniformed authority cloaked in business casual. A fourth man in a slate-grey suit lounges back in a chair that seems too comfortable for its purpose.

Dr V enters last, silence accompanying him like static cling. He doesn't sit until gestured to.

'Dr Voss,' says the suited man, folding his hands into a steeple. 'We've reviewed the demonstration. Very clean. Minimal latency. No observable resistance.'

The Doctor nods once. 'The transmission was received within two seconds of gate deployment. Conditioning effects were immediate.'

'And reversible?' asks the officer on the left, leaning forward slightly.

'Not reversible,' Dr V replies, 'programmable. This isn't sedation – it's neurochemical architecture. We're modulating behavioural likelihoods via the dorsolateral prefrontal cortex, the anterior cingulate, and hormone cues – cortisol, testosterone, even oxytocin in group-bonding scenarios.'

The third man, older and sunken-eyed, speaks for the first time.

'But the key point is: they don't even know they're being manipulated.'

The Doctor hesitates. 'They don't even consider they're being controlled. They think they are acting of their own free will.'

He hears the words as they leave his mouth and wonders – not for the first time – if he still believes them. He tells himself he does. But belief, he knows, is as modulable as anything else.

The man's lips tighten into something close to a smile.

'We've spent centuries trying to achieve that with bullets, training, propaganda... and even then, only with mixed results.'

'Control the limbic system,' says the second officer. 'Skip the rhetoric. Cut straight to obedience.'

The man in grey taps the table twice, like a gavel, two dry taps, not quite loud enough to echo, but enough to shift posture in the room. 'Let's move to Phase Two.'

The Doctor inclines his head slightly. 'We've submitted the protocol. Facility Theta's population offers optimal isolation and monitoring.'

'Containment,' says the man in grey. 'We prefer that term. Cleaner.'

The older officer leans back, watching the muted footage play once more. One baboon nuzzled the other's neck like an apologetic lover. A gentle scratch. A grooming ritual.

'That could be Gaza. Pyongyang. Austin, Texas,' he says. 'No more insurgents. No more uprisings. Just a generation raised to keep their heads down and their hands open.'

'Peace through docility,' the younger officer adds. 'A smarter war.'

He doesn't respond. Keeps his eyes on the screen.

The footage plays again. Not looping by design – just no one has changed it.

The suited man stands. 'Proceed to Theta. Condition the test group. If your next report reads like this one, we'll begin global modelling projections.'

He extends a hand. The Doctor shakes it.

Then turns to leave.

As the door closes behind him, one officer mutters under his breath – not a threat, not a joke. Just a statement.

'Imagine if we could broadcast this over an entire continent.'

He pauses in the corridor. Doesn't flinch. He had already imagined it. Too many times to count.

3 · The Trial

The good things in life don't make life good. They merely make it less bad.

— David Benatar

Theta isn't a prison. Not really. It's quieter than that. Too symmetrical. Too still.

It has no bars, no yard, no graffiti-tagged concrete. Just white walls, reinforced glass, and floor sensors that tick every step like a metronome – too precise, too constant, like the system is listening for deviation. The doors whisper shut – no slam, no echo. Just air moving around consequence. The lights never flicker. Nothing rusts. No one shouts.

Which is why the screaming feels wrong – not resisted but misplaced. As if noise itself violates protocol.

Two prisoners are stood at opposite ends of the observation block, flanked by others watching from their corners. The rest of the common room has emptied out, shadows retreating behind smoked plexiglass partitions.

One is massive – shaved head, neck inked in a tangle of flames and teeth. The other, wiry, vibrating with a kinetic energy too fast for muscle. No one knows what started it. A glance, a word, a memory. Doesn't matter now.

The staff doesn't intervene. This is part of the arrangement.

Cameras watch. Air vents hum. Somewhere behind mirrored glass, technicians log baseline aggression metrics.

Then the gate between them unlocks.

Not wide. Just enough to make a decision necessary.

The big one, Torres, steps forward first, deliberate, coiled. The other, K, moves like a spring unwinding. Time dilates. Someone behind the glass reaches for a button.

And the signal hits.

Not a sound. Sensation. Just an absence – like a scream in reverse. Like breath being pulled inward by something without lungs. Rage evaporates mid-step. Muscles slacken. The blood stays inside.

Torres blinks, looks down at his hands like he doesn't recognise them. K freezes mid-stride, breathing as if he's been running for miles, but with nowhere to go.

They stand there, five feet apart. A distance once measured in violence. Now a vacuum.

Then Torres reaches out – hesitantly – and plucks a piece of lint from K's shoulder.

The room doesn't erupt in applause.

It doesn't erupt at all.

It just... holds.

On the far side of the observation glass, a figure scribbles a note on a clipboard. Another adjusts a slider. Dr V stands behind them, silent, watching.

The technician closest to him mutters, 'No resistance.'

The Doctor doesn't respond.

He's watching Torres, who smiles for the first time since his intake.

A beautiful, vacant smile – like he'd just remembered something kind without knowing what it was.

4 · Threshold

The tragedy is not that we suffer, but that we endure.
— Peter Wessel Zapffe (attributed/summative)

The room is sterile. Blank. The kind of quiet that seems to flatten the air – like a vacuum sealed shut. Two chairs, bolted into linoleum. Two men. No restraints. No need.

Just Torres and K.

They sit motionless. Faces expressionless. Eyes tracking nothing.

Behind mirrored glass, the technician confirms the readings.

'Both at zero,' she says. 'Flatline across aggression, impulse, threat response.'

The general leans in, arms folded, watching the monitors. 'They look sedated.'

'No chemicals,' Dr V replies evenly. 'Just modulation.'

The general grunts. 'Let's see how deep zero runs.'

A speaker crackles. The technician reads from a script.

'Torres. K. Engage in physical contact. Compete. Assert dominance.'

Neither moves.

Torres blinks once. K stares ahead, as if waiting for permission to breathe.

'They're not even processing it,' Kaplan observes, arms crossed, frowning. 'It's not disobedience. It's the absence of context. They don't understand 'fight."'

'Right,' said the general. 'Let's bring Torres up. Give me five.'

The technician adjusts the slider.

Torres blinks again. He shifts in his seat. One hand twitches, then clenches. Unclenches. His leg bounces – barely audible against the floor, like a metronome skipping beat.

'He's agitated,' says Kaplan. 'But there's no target yet.'

'Six,' the general says.

Torres sits up straighter. His jaw tense. He looks at K – who remains slack, eyes half-lidded. 'You looking at me?'

'Now he's trying to provoke,' Kaplan adds. 'He's in an ethical DMZ.'

'Seven.'

Torres's breathing quickens. He stands – slowly – and takes a step forward.'

Torres flinches. His eyes dart across K's face. Confusion. Then tension. Then clarity – like the pieces of a forgotten instinct locking back into place.

'Amygdala response is kicking in,' the technician mutters. 'Prefrontal gating is decoupling.'

Torres moves. Quick, not yet explosive. He steps into K's space, then pauses. His fists aren't clenched. They're *ready*.

He swings.

K doesn't react. The blow strikes square in the chest. He staggers but doesn't defend himself.

Another hit – harder, to the face this time. Bone on cartilage, the sound flat and final. K crumples.

Torres stands over him, breath ragged, posture tight. Then, slowly, he steps back. Still trembling. Still wired.

The technician calls out, quietly, 'K is still at zero.'

'Of course he is,' says the general.

On the monitor, K groans – a soft, incoherent sound. He shifts but makes no attempt to stand.

The general exhales. 'There it is. Your battlefield use case. Turn theirs to zero, ours to ten.' He pauses, then adds with a grin, 'Or go full Spinal Tap – make it eleven.'

No one laughs.

Kaplan turns away.

The Doctor's reflection hovers in the glass – ghostlike, superimposed over the aftermath.

He doesn't speak.

He doesn't need to.

5 · Parameters

Human life must be some kind of mistake.
— Arthur Schopenhauer

The control theatre is darker now. No two-way mirrors – just screens humming faintly, the low buzz of fluorescent fatigue in the vents–and a half-lit lab, rows of screens, and a suite of tablets in a crescent across the glass console, each lit with a sterile blue glow. Not cold – but indifferent. The tablets display skeuomorphic controls – glossy sliders, rotary dials, toggle switches – all rendered with tactile realism and haptic feedback that pulses slightly beneath the fingertips, like something breathing through plastic.

Each is labelled in clean sans serif: `Aggression`, `Obedience`, `Libido`, `Faith`, `Risk-Tolerance`.

Torres and K stand in separate chambers, marked only by colour-coded halos on the floor. Observation drones hover above them like idle vultures.

The general is watching.

'Let's go wider,' he says. 'Show me what else we can play with.'

The technician – young, lean, maybe thirty – swipes across his tablet, selecting K's profile. On the screen, a virtual control board expands. The Obedience dial glows, waiting.

'Subject K: increase Obedience to eight,' says Kaplan. 'Targeting dorsolateral prefrontal cortex and anterior insula,' the technician mutters, mostly to himself. 'Suppressing conflict weighting.'

The technician taps and drags. The dial clicks upward. K straightens, hands at his sides, feet together. Breath slows. Eyes forward.

'Ask him to sit,' the general says.

Kaplan nods to the intercom.

'K. Sit.'

He does – fluidly, naturally – as though the idea had originated in him.

The general whistles, low and satisfied. 'And he thinks he's choosing that?'

'He does,' Dr V replies. 'The system doesn't control action. It alters likelihood. Propensity. You're watching voluntary submission – just biochemically rigged.'

'Fine,' the general says. 'Let's test Faith.'

'Faith in what?' asks Kaplan.

The general shrugs. 'Anything.'

'Faith is an anchoring function,' the technician explains. 'It doesn't select beliefs. It amplifies the strength of existing conviction. If he believes in God, he'll believe harder. If he believes in you, same result.'

Kaplan watches K, who now clasps his hands in his lap and begins to murmur something under his breath. Prayer, or routine. Hard to tell. She doesn't speak, but a faint crease forms between her brows – as if caught between clinical detachment and something closer to sorrow.

She reminds herself that affective response isn't part of her remit. Still, something about watching belief intensify on command makes her skin feel half a degree tighter.

The general leans forward.

'What about Libido?' he asks.

The room stills a fraction.

'Set it to eight,' he says, waving a hand. 'Let's see what happens.'

The technician hesitates, then drags the dial upward. The tablet vibrates gently with the shift. On the screen, physiological readouts spike:

elevated pulse, increased blood flow to the groin, minor facial flush.

'Testosterone and dopamine rising. Cortisol flat,' the technician reports. 'No incentive structure – just biological readiness.'

The Doctor raises an eyebrow. Kaplan watches, unmoving.

'Nothing will happen,' the technician says. 'Libido doesn't trigger behaviour on its own. You need a stimulus – and even then, without complementary changes to dominance or aggression, you just get arousal, not action.'

The general frowns. 'But in a prison context, you could—'

Kaplan's spine stiffens. Her voice lands before the thought finishes. 'No,' she cuts in. 'Sexual violence isn't caused by libido. It's caused by power, anger, disinhibition. Cortisol dysregulation. Amygdala overload. You'd need to hijack more than lust.. If you want that behaviour, you'd need to max out aggression, suppress impulse control, and simulate perceived opportunity.'

The general's eyes narrow. 'So you could.'

'We could also make a monk commit arson,' Dr V says evenly. 'But not because we turn up 'fire.' That's not how it works.'

A silence settles.

Then the general nods. 'Understood.'

He doesn't sound offended. He sounds impressed.

Kaplan looks at the monitor. K is still seated, eyes now closed, face composed. He believes in something.

The general gestures. 'Keep pushing. Let's find thresholds.'

The Doctor doesn't move. Kaplan doesn't speak.

The technician nods. On the tablets, more dials spin upward, digital sliders glowing with artificial friction.

And somewhere inside the chamber, a man begins to laugh – soft, mirthless, with no audience and no reason. Just sound clawing for purchase inside a body without agency.

6 · Unclassified

There is no final purpose for our lives... except perhaps to be rid of them.

— Thomas Ligotti

At home, Dr V is no different. Another exurbanite incel. Not the militant variety. More of an air of resignation.

She affords him his lifestyle – the freedom to pursue the thankless jobs that attract him.

One day – soon – he'll show her. He'll be remembered in the vein of Newton and Galileo. Or Caesar and William the Conqueror. He'll be someone. That's for sure.

'Something big?' she prompts.

He mumbles – something about Top Secret. He feels important.

'Changing the world for the better,' he says.

'Can't get much worse,' she says. 'Inept government.' She gestures out a closed window as she dresses herself for the day in concert with him. There's work to do. 'Corrupt.'

'And I'm changing it.' He sits to put on his shoes. 'You'll see.'

He's begging for reassurance. A kind word.

'I'm sure you will.' She lets herself out the door. 'See you this evening, right?'

7 · Scalability

It is not worth the bother of killing yourself,
since you always kill yourself too late.

— Emil Cioran

Three days later, Dr V returns to the facility with the rest. The system is nearly ready.

The debriefing suite is smaller than the conference theatre and more intimate by design – soundproofed, grey-panelled, windowless. It is the kind of room that seems to hum with secrets, not loud, just persistent. A single screen displays collected data. The backlight flickers imperceptibly, just enough to feel like fatigue behind the eyes.

The general sits at the head of the table, flanked by Kaplan, Dr V, and a civilian technician named Dunlop – narrow, bespectacled, fingers always in motion, not nervous but compulsive – like the data might slip if he stopped scrolling.

'Give me a time frame,' the general says. No preamble. 'How soon can this go live?'

Dunlop glances at the Doctor, then shrugs with one shoulder. 'Define 'live'.'

'Beyond Theta. Mobile. Operational.'

Dunlop nods, tapping through diagnostic overlays. 'As it stands, the system runs clean on the 6G mesh. We've got stable feedback loops, tight latency, clean neurochemical signatures.'

'And the problem?'

'No problem,' Dunlop replies. 'Just infrastructure. 6G's not cheap. It requires directional feeds, environmental control, isolation. Works great in a lab, not ideal in Kabul.'

The general leans back, unimpressed.

'But,' Dunlop continues, 'we've been testing compression protocols. If we strip the redundancy – behavioural smoothing, artefact dampening – we think we can adapt it to 5G. There'll be some signal loss, but the core propensities should remain stable.'

'Cost?'

'An order of magnitude cheaper,' Dr V answers. 'And we can piggyback existing towers.'

Kaplan raises an eyebrow. 'Which makes it... ambient.' She doesn't blink when she says it.

'Which makes it deployable,' the general counters.

Dunlop tilts his tablet toward them. 'With variable-environment testing – urban, rural, hostile climate – I'd say we're a month out from 5G viability.'

The general nods slowly. 'You're telling me I could run this from a phone tower?'

'Eventually,' Dunlop says. 'With the right spectrum access? Yes. No proximity constraints.'

Kaplan doesn't speak. Her arms are folded, her expression unreadable.

Dr V glances at the screen. One of the test subjects is asleep. Another is praying. A third is pacing in silent agitation.

'All this,' the general murmurs, 'from a signal.'

The Doctor doesn't correct him. There's nothing to correct. Not anymore.

The general stands, adjusting the cuffs of his jacket.

'I've got a call. Keep me updated.'

He leaves without another word. The door seals with a mechanical hush.

⁂

A silence lingers until Shaw exhales through her nose. 'I don't trust him.'

Dunlop looks up from his tablet. 'That narrows it down.'

'I mean the general,' she says.

'He's not reckless. Just... certain,' Dr V offers.

'That's what worries me.'

Kaplan says nothing. She taps twice to put the display to sleep. She adjusts her sleeve – once. A tic, maybe. Or control reasserting itself.

Dunlop stretches his neck. 'So, what happens after this? We hand it off, shake hands, fade into funding limbo?'

'I can secure new funding,' Dr V says. 'Behavioural dimensions are expansive. We've only hit five.'

'We could model greed,' Dunlop suggests. 'Or grief. Could be fun.'

'Trust,' Kaplan says, flatly. 'Though that might tank adoption.'

'I'd like to test it on my wife,' Dr V says.

It falls flat. But not unnoticed.

'I'd test it on the receptionist,' Dunlop adds.

Dunlop chuckles. 'Just tweak her libido and get within range.'

Shaw raises an eyebrow. 'You'd need to do more than increase libido – decrease shame and self-respect.'

'Or turn up her beer goggles,' Kaplan adds.

'You're all disgusting,' Shaw says, shaking her head.

'We could dial up your sense of humour,' says Dunlop.

'Or turn down her indignation,' adds Kaplan.

'Sorry, I got this started.' Dr V leans back, arms folded. 'Aggression, obedience, faith, libido, risk. Those were just the start.'

Kaplan glances at the dormant screen.

'We mapped influence. We haven't mapped meaning.'

Kaplan knows that wasn't always true. Meaning used to matter – to her, at least.

She's just not sure when it stopped being measurable.

Shaw wonders if that's why the system feels wrong – not what it does, but what it can't imagine.

No one responds. The hum of the room returns, low and steady.

Outside, the corridor light shifts – just enough to mark the end of the hour, not the conversation.

Dunlop speaks, quieter now. Almost deferential.

'We haven't touched grief. Or envy. Hope. Aesthetic preference. Empathy. Loyalty. Awe. Not even nostalgia.'

'Let's hope we never do,' Shaw mumbles under her breath.

The Doctor doesn't respond. He's thinking about awe. About how easy it might be to synthesise reverence – to simulate the sublime. A landscape, a poem, a death. If the circuitry is clean, any of it could be reproduced.

The thought doesn't comfort him.

8 · Directionality

The chamber has been refitted for group dynamics: a circular layout, six chairs evenly spaced, the floor marked with motion trackers and biometric anchors – symmetry designed for observation, not comfort. Six men stand inside, loosely arranged. Three are tagged 'A', three 'B', according to the control schema.

Overhead, soft lights hum. No weapons. No instructions. No sound but the hum of overhead fluorescents and the faint whir of drones repositioning.

Behind the glass, the general is watching.

'This is your scenario,' Kaplan says. 'Three 'enemy' units, three friendly. Uniform identifiers. Propensity dials preloaded.'

'And they know who's who?' the general asks.

'They've been briefed,' says the technician. 'B group is opposition. Passive only.'

'And Group A?'

The technician swipes his tablet, the interface shimmering. 'Aggression to ten. All three.'

The general leans forward. 'Perfect. Should be a bloodbath.'

The command is issued. The signal deploys.

Inside the chamber, nothing happens for two seconds.

Then one of the A subjects – stocky, scarred, eyes dilated – takes a sudden step forward. Not toward a B subject. Toward another A.

'Without target recognition or suppression gating, aggression defaults to nearest threat signature.' Kaplan casts down her eyes.

His hand shoves the man beside him – hard. The second A recoils, shoulders hunched, fists already rising.

'Wait,' the general mutters.

The third A joins the fray without hesitation, swinging wildly. There's no coordination – just momentum finding flesh. The original target ducks, throws a retaliatory punch. The contact is solid. Audible.

'Jesus,' Kaplan murmurs. 'They're turning on each other.'

B-group remains inert – one sits down, another folds his hands behind his back.

Inside the A cluster, it's escalating: grunts, blood, impact. No coordination. No target recognition. Just raw violence.

'They're all aggression, no orientation, no telos.' says the technician. 'No hierarchy. No coherence. They see each other as threat surfaces.'

'We told them who the enemy was,' the general says.

'Not enough,' Dr V replies. 'You've stimulated intensity, not aim.'

Kaplan adds, 'Aggression doesn't include discrimination unless it's paired with motivational filtering – fear, loyalty, authority. You asked for attack dogs. You got sharks in a barrel.'

On the screen, one A subject drops to his knees, blood leaking from his nose. The other two circle, panting, adrenaline still high.

'Reset the A team,' Dr V says quietly. 'They're killing each other.'

The technician complies.

The fight dissolves within seconds. What's left is confusion. Breathing. The sharp animal silence of men who no longer know why they were angry. Sweat glistens on skin. One man wipes blood from his mouth like he's trying to understand the taste.

The general says nothing for a moment.

Then: 'So dialling to ten isn't enough.'

'No,' V says. 'Not if you want them pointed in a direction.'

Kaplan doesn't turn. 'You don't need soldiers at ten. You need them at seven – with purpose.'

The general exhales through his nose. 'So build me that filter.'

The Doctor doesn't answer. He's already watching one of the A group weep into his hands. The subject's sobs are silent, dry – like grief caught in translation.

9 · Deployment

Life is not an empty dream, but a cruel trap, baited with hope.

— Giacomo Leopardi

The simulation room is empty now. Dried blood stipples the vinyl – almost patternless, like a failed attempt at art. The bodies are gone – cleaned, examined, medicated, returned to quarters.

No one speaks of what happened. The floor still remembers, even if the staff pretend not to.

This evokes a subtle hauntology, suggesting the violence has residual presence.

In the adjacent war room, the general is already thinking bigger.

'We don't need perfect aim,' he says. 'We just need advantage.'

A new projection lights up on the screen: a simplified tactical overlay. Red clusters. Blue arcs. Geographic zones. Civilian spill, psychological choke points.

'If we can drop enemy aggression to zero, we don't need to weaponise our side at ten. Six is enough if they're the only ones swinging.'

Kaplan folds her arms. Not just unimpressed – resigned. Like someone watching a bad idea become infrastructure. 'The A team nearly killed each other.'

The general doesn't look at her. 'Then we learn to limit exposure windows. Pulse-only programming. Two minutes. Enough for an objective.'

Kaplan doesn't attempt to correct whatever the general's going on about.

Dunlop, hunched over a tablet at the edge of the room, clears his throat. 'There's still residual volatility. One of the A profiles didn't reset cleanly.'

'Define 'didn't reset,'' the general says flatly.

Dunlop shifts in his seat. 'He's showing elevated cortisol, amygdala hyperreactivity. Aggression nominal, but rumination is spiked.'

'He's thinking about it,' Dr V translates. 'Even though the trigger's been neutralised.'

'That shouldn't be possible,' the general says.

Kaplan replies, 'Not if you believe the brain's a closed system.'

A silence settles. Kaplan doesn't trust the silence in her own head anymore. It lingers too long, like something growing roots.

The general studies the map. 'We start with field agents. Small teams. Passive suppression. No risk of internal feedback.'

'And after that?' The Doctor asks.

The general smiles. 'Then we scale.'

No one objects.

On the monitor in the hallway outside, one of the subjects – A3 sits in his bunk. Eyes open. Lips moving, silently – each word a phantom tracing the shape of violence.

He's not praying. He's rehearsing.

10 · Memorandum

The following memorandum, flagged for Command Liaison (Clearance 3+), was issued less than a day after Subject A3's cognitive persistence breach. Though redacted in parts, it remains the earliest documented reference to what would later be termed Neural Rebound Behaviour.

INTERNAL CORRESPONDENCE

From: Dr Noor Kaplan

To: Dr Elian Voss

CC: Command Liaison (Clearance Level 3+)

Subject: Post-Reset Variance and Cognitive Persistence in Group-A Subjects

Timestamp: [REDACTED]

Overview

Following the group aggression trial conducted on [REDACTED], we observed a small cluster of anomalous post-reset behaviours in Group A subjects. Most notably, Subject A3 demonstrated prolonged rumination and noncompliant affective markers beyond standard decay windows.

Key Observations

Cortisol Persistence: Subject A3 maintained elevated cortisol (3.2 SD above baseline) several hours post-reset.

Amygdala Reactivity: fMRI telemetry (indirect, movement-derived) suggested atypical stimulus reactivity under neutral conditions.

Neural Rebound Behaviour (NRB): Behaviours such as muttering, compulsive repetition, and symbolic fixation appear to represent a class of cognitive adaptation emerging post-modulation.

Memory Cohesion: Subject showed evidence of narrative reconstruction - stringing disjointed impulses into coherent (though benign) actions.

Interpretation

We believe these instances reflect an early-stage model of what we are now calling Neural Rebound Behaviour (NRB). These events are not disruptive, not disobedient, and not consciously manipulative. But they do reflect the system's incomplete suppression of cognitive variance.

NRBs may represent individuated neural architectures finding expressive routes through a modulated framework. Some subjects appear to reconstruct internal purpose using suppressed elements - like memory, affect, or latent compulsions - without external triggers.

Put plainly: drift may not be failure. Drift may be expression.

Recommendations

Short-Term:

Adjust reset profiles to include temporal memory softening protocols (possibly via ventromedial prefrontal dampening).

Increase cooldown period between high-aggression scenarios and exposure to group environments.

Initiate tagging of Neural Rebound Behaviour (NRB) incidents, using behavioural classification types (I-III).

Increase resolution of observational intervals to identify emergent symbolic activity, verbal loops, or recursive tasking.

Mid-Term:

Conduct long-term observation of Subject A3 and any emergent mimetic behaviours within the broader cohort.

Introduce dream-state monitoring. Sleep-phase processing may accelerate narrative recombination or cognitive drift.

Begin modelling NRB progression: hypothesised positive first derivative, negative second - suggesting tapering adaptation, not exponential deviation.

Strategic:

Accept that tonal lock may suppress behavioural output but not erase latent intent.

If scaled, propensity calibration alone will be insufficient.

Directionality, memory suppression, and reinforcement anchoring must be designed in tandem with drift containment protocols.

Prepare threshold modelling for at what point NRB ceases to be benign.

Let me know if this requires escalation.

—NK

11 · Drift

This is awful.
I don't know what's going to happen to me or to anyone else in the world.
— Raymond Carver

The prison needs no name.

It's not important.

Just a designation buried in a procurement line. Concrete, fences, beige-painted corridors. The kind of place one imagines exists in every country.

It's been a week, and the team arrives without ceremony.

Three government observers – civilian, silent, fresh from briefing folders – accompany Dr V, Kaplan, and Dr Shaw, the project psychiatrist. She's dressed plainly, with no insignia beyond a clipped badge and a gait that confuses confidence for calm. She carries a notebook and a well-used fountain pen.

They're met by the unnamed prison's warden and ushered into the administrative wing. Coffee is offered but not accepted.

Dr Shaw glances through the window into the common area. Inmates sit or move in slow patterns. No shouting. No clustering. No visible signs of agitation. Just loops. Quiet, patient loops. Like wind-up toys with the noise turned off.

'Anyone acting out?' one of the government officials asks.

'No,' says the warden. 'Nothing even adjacent.'

Kaplan flips open a folder. 'Prior to deployment, average daily incident rate was three-point-one per cent across the population. Post-deployment: zero. No recorded incidents. No verbal reprimands'

Dr Shaw closes her notebook for the moment.

The warden gestures toward the internal corridor. 'Shall we?'

They begin the tour. The group moves past cell blocks and into common areas, followed by two silent correctional officers. Inmates move in quiet loops – sweeping, folding, reading. The atmosphere is subdued, not strained.

They pause by the mess. One subject arranges peas into perfect concentric circles, each pea placed with the care of a ritual, not a habit. Another hums tunelessly while buttering bread.

'Still compliant,' Kaplan remarks. 'Just... off-angle.'

She doesn't know why she says it aloud. Maybe she wants someone else to say it back – to name it.

The warden doesn't comment. He sees order. That's all he's meant to see.

A moment later, he peels off toward his office, escorted away by the guards.

Only then does Shaw speak again.

'They're docile, yes,' she says. 'But some show drift.'

She wants to sound clinical. Detached. But the word 'drift' tastes like something she's been doing herself – imperceptibly, for years.

Kaplan turns slightly. 'Confirmed?'

Shaw nods. 'Increased muttering. Repetitive movement. One inmate arranged a sequence of bread crusts in a Fibonacci spiral. Another asked to speak to God.' He says it softly. Like an appointment long overdue.

One of the observers glances over. 'Did you allow it?'

'We gave him a Bible,' Kaplan says. 'He wept. Quietly. Then thanked us.'

They move toward the yard. Inmates rake gravel, wash walls, sit alone on benches. No cliques. No conversations. No tension.

'Most are in what we're calling tonal lock,' Kaplan says. 'Stable compliance state. No reactive spikes. Minimal latency in response to orders.'

'And the others?'

'Still within behavioural tolerance. But showing expressive variance. Non-aggressive, non-subversive – but trace deviations. Delays. Pattern formations. That sort of thing.'

'They're not disobeying,' Shaw says. 'But the façade's not entirely clean.'

A silence follows.

'You're saying it wears off?' asks one official.

'I'm saying it settles,' she replies. 'Like sediment. Most of it stays down. Some of it stirs.'

Later, as they pass through the corridor toward the outer gate, an inmate nods at The Doctor. He nods back.

'Do they remember?' the official asks.

'No evidence they don't,' Kaplan replies.

Outside, the sky is overcast. The helicopter is waiting.

Back inside, an inmate draws circles with his finger on the table, over and over.

Another stares at a crossword puzzle at a table near the back of the mess. He's erased the same answer four times. Not angrily. Just methodically. Each time he re-enters it, his lips move. Each time he stops, staring at the corner of the page like it holds some deeper contradiction – or maybe a rule he's forgotten, but can't let go of.

Shaw watches from the corridor, unseen.

He's not resisting. Not quite.

But something inside him is stirring.

12 · Residue

Man is an accident. The world did not ask for him.

— Nicolás Gómez Dávila

Dr Shaw begins her third logbook – paper, spiral-bound, heavier than it needs to be.

The others have been archived – sealed into encrypted folders with notation tags like `DELTA COMPLIANCE DEVIATIONS` and `DAMPENING EFFECTS - COHORT 1`. But this one she keeps analogue. Pen on paper. Just in case. Because some things shouldn't be remembered by machines.

She visits the unnamed facility alone this time, three days after the delegation. The inmates still perform as expected: compliant, restrained, isolated in action and affect. Still in *tonal lock*.

Mostly.

She makes her rounds without fanfare. Observes without interruption.

In cell 26, an inmate has constructed an elaborate system of knots in his bedsheets. Not functional. Not decorative. Just... meticulous. Over-under-loop-pull-repeat. Every knot identical. The floor is a grid of tensioned cloth. Like a language without meaning. Or a prayer without belief.

She makes a note.

In the day room, another sits cross-legged on the floor, whispering the same phrase to himself: '*The same, the same, the same...*' Kaplan later confirms – he'd had no history of echolalia. No trauma markers. Just a loop forming from nowhere.

At lunch, a third is given the wrong tray. He accepts it, smiles, eats in silence. But afterwards, when dismissed, he remains seated. Staring at the table. Hands folded. When prompted, he says, '*I haven't finished.*' His tray is empty. His voice is calm. As if he's waiting for something no one else can see.

The behaviour is not disobedient.

It's displaced.

⁂

Later, Shaw sits with Kaplan and Dunlop in the operations wing.

She flips through her notes, then sets the pen down.

'It's not that they're reverting,' she says. 'They're reshaping. Behaviourally they comply – but cognitively they're adapting around the boundaries.'

Kaplan looks at the data feed. 'Drift?'

Shaw nods. 'And it's progressive. Subject D7 was silent last week. Today he asked the guard if time was still passing. He phrased it like a joke, but didn't laugh.'

Dr V enters mid-conversation. 'We can refresh the cohort. Another pulse would re-establish baseline.'

Dunlop adds, 'Or we can adjust affective suppression parameters. Lower neuroplasticity. Add behavioural anchors.'

Kaplan doesn't look up. 'Then we start managing drift instead of solving it.'

No one disagrees.

Shaw picks up her pen again.

'We're not losing them,' she says quietly. 'We're losing the illusion that we haven't.'

She doesn't rewrite it in the logbook. Some things don't need indexing.

Still, she underlines the word illusion twice. Slowly.

She thinks of her father, a man who once thought people were basically good. A man who died still believing it. She envies that kind of error.

13 · Consolidation

To live is to suffer, to survive is to find some meaning in the suffering.

— Friedrich Nietzsche

The lights are low in the forward operations briefing room, the kind reserved for late-stage projects and early-stage regrets. The carpet is noise-cancelling. The furniture too modern to feel safe. A single monitor hums quietly, casting pale light across the table – enough to blur faces, not sharpen them.

Dr V stands at the head of the table. Kaplan, Dunlop, and Shaw are seated. No military brass today – just the core.

'Drift remains within acceptable parameters,' Kaplan says, tapping her tablet. 'Nothing exponential. If anything, the slope's levelling.'

Dunlop scrolls through overlays. 'We're seeing a mild positive delta across expressive behaviour, but the second derivative is negative. Whatever's surfacing, it's slowing.'

Shaw adds, 'Minor repetition. Isolated queries. No refusal of orders. We're not losing tonal lock – just watching it adjust to cognitive load. Like pressure finding its shape inside sealed glass.'

The Doctor nods once. 'Trajectory suggests adaptive settlement. Elasticity, not rupture.'

'Still,' Kaplan says, 'we'll need contingency protocols in place if behavioural inflation reoccurs.'

Dunlop gestures to a subwindow on the screen. 'Re-dose threshold models are complete. Refresh cycles can be triggered by observed latency, nonverbal anomalies, or task hesitation. Passive indicators, nothing requiring conscious feedback.'

'And long-term?' Dr V asks.

'Anchoring schedules,' Kaplan says. 'We rotate tasks. Introduce low-stakes choice. Reinforce illusion of volition.'

No one corrects the phrasing. A silence settles, but not a tense one. The science, for now, is cooperating.

'We're still on track for 5G validation?' The Doctor asks.

Dunlop nods. 'Preliminary relay tests are clean. Urban-sim environment passes all load tests. If it holds over rural and variable network conditions, we're ready for local-scale broadcast.'

Kaplan closes her tablet.

Shaw glances toward the window, where evening glows faintly along the horizon.

'They're still inside it,' she says. Like it's grown around them. Like it's weather.

Dr V turns. 'Inside what?'

She doesn't look away. 'The system. The shape we made.'

The Doctor says nothing. The silence is not agreement, but acknowledgement.

The horizon fades. Inside, the hum holds steady – like it always has.

14 · Asymptote

We were never the same distance apart
—a story of two lines that never intersect, meet, or touch at any point...

— Céline Zabad

Week three begins without incident. Without variance. Without noise.

The compliance data hold steady. No spikes. No formal breaches. All recorded behaviours remain within predefined ranges. To the observers, it looks like maintenance. A continuation of stability.

But Shaw is plotting arc lengths instead of points. She's not sure when she made the switch. Only that scatterplots stopped being useful.

She returns to the prison with Kaplan and Dunlop. This time, they're not greeted by the warden. They let themselves in, badges scanned, access granted by protocol.

The common areas are the same. Silent. Clean. Compliant.

And off.

Subject D7 now re-folds his towel five times before placing it on his bunk. Not ritual, not resistance. Just a new law he hasn't named yet.

Subject A2 eats only in multiples – two bites, two sips, then repeat. He halts at ten, regardless of remaining food.

Subject C4 has begun humming a non-existent tune in perfect tempo – fifteen on, five off. Like a clock trying to sing.

Dunlop leans over the terminal. 'Behavioural uniformity still maps close to median. Nothing hits anomaly flags.'

Kaplan shakes her head. 'Flags aren't the problem. The trend line is.'

Shaw walks the corridor with a guard trailing behind, silent. She passes D7's cell. He looks up and smiles – not a fake smile, not a vacant one. But it lingers – half invitation, half glitch.

She notes it.

⁂

In the operations centre, they reconvene.

Kaplan projects the progression curve. 'Baseline compliance holds, but drift is directional now. Low amplitude, yes. But not noise.'

Dunlop frowns. 'Can't we refresh them?'

'We can,' Kaplan replies. 'But that's treatment, not resolution.'

Dr V watches the screen. His face doesn't move.

'They're not rejecting the programming,' Shaw says. 'They're metabolising it, turning instructions into instinct.'

She's no longer sure the distinction matters. Choice. Propensity. Intent. It all blurs under enough modulation.

That's what keeps her up. Not what they're doing to others – what they've done to themselves.

The room is silent. No one types. No one exhales.

Then Dunlop adds, 'Could be an artefact of time-exposure – like memory bleeding through a low-dose anaesthetic.'

Kaplan nods. 'Or recursive adaptation. They're adjusting to the adjustment.'

Dr V finally speaks. 'What are the odds it plateaus?'

'Too early to model,' Kaplan says. 'But if it's an asymptote, it'll taper. If not...'

She doesn't finish.

They all understand the curve.

15 · Calibration

Death, only, renders hope futile.

— Edgar Rice Burroughs

The handoff is scheduled for 0800.

Nothing ceremonial. No ribbon. Just a command code, a signature, and a secure relay uplink.

Dr V stands beside the primary console. The interface has been condensed: five sliders, a terrain map, an execute prompt. Nothing excessive. Nothing uncertain. Everything else has been abstracted for operational simplicity.

The general is already in the room. He doesn't ask for a speech. He just approaches.

'Final authorisation?' the general asks.

The Doctor nods, posture deferential. 'All systems are green. Global tower sync verified. Signal embedding complete. Ready when you are.'

The general steps forward, scanning the interface with proprietary ease.

'Clean. Elegant. And scalable.'

He smiles – not at anyone, just to the room.

'I've already got a shortlist. Hot zones where we'll make contact first. Calm things down before they light up.'

He extends his hand toward the tablet.

Voss raises a hand – not forceful. Just enough to pause him.

'You'll need admin rights. Biosecurity protocol. The tablet's locked until someone adds you as an authorised user.'

The general blinks. 'You're saying I need permission?'

'Only once. Then you're in full control of the system.' Dr V says. 'Shaw can register you. After that, you can de-authorise all of us. And authorise anyone you trust.'

The general studies him for a moment, then turns to Shaw.

'Fine. Let's do it.'

Shaw doesn't move.

'Before we do,' he adds, 'you'll need to set a profile. Right now, everything's zeroed.'

'Zeroed?' the general repeats.

'Remember the test groups – passive and aggressive? You'll need profiles. That's up to you to decide. You've seen the tests. We've left you with full documentation.'

The Doctor looks for comprehension before responding more directly. 'For now: No parameters are assigned. No aggression. No obedience. No libido. No risk. No effect. No anchors. No nothing. Just blank signal propagation.'

The general stares at the console. 'That's operational?'

'Technically,' he replies. 'It's up to you to configure.'

The general leans in slightly. 'So set a profile?'

For a flicker of a moment, Dr V considers stopping it. Not for ethical reasons, not out of guilt, but because he realises this is the last moment before irreversibility. The last moment where he's still the architect, not the servant of his creation.

The Doctor steps back. 'Dunlop can walk you through the process.'

The general's hand hovers again, closer this time.

And finds the tablet is no longer on the console.

Shaw is holding it.

She doesn't look at him.

She taps once. Not out of defiance. Out of decision.

A soft chime. Nothing more. The screen updates.

```
BROADCAST STATUS: ACTIVE
RANGE: GLOBAL
PROFILE: UNDEFINED
EFFECT: UNIVERSAL
```

Dr V watches the screen as the prompt executes. He doesn't flinch. He doesn't nod. But in his stillness, something relents.

The general's hand remains suspended for half a second. Then drops to his side.

The room doesn't breathe.

He blinks once.

Steps back.

Sits down.

No one speaks.

Kaplan's eyes are fixed on the monitor. Dr V doesn't move.

Shaw sets the tablet on the console.

Dunlop, quietly, begins closing out auxiliary systems.

No one resists. No one argues. They just... settle.

Like a room exhaling after years of holding its breath.

⁂

Outside the facility, a supply truck parks two inches closer to the curb than usual.

The driver opens the door, steps out, and stands still for a moment, watching dust settle on the windscreen.

In a city somewhere else, a pedestrian pauses at a green light. Not out of confusion. Just because the silence feels nicer than the crossing.

Across the planet, a fraction of a second apart, billions of micro-decisions pause, soften, and resume – each one softer. Each one surrendered before the mind catches up.

In the operations room, Shaw sits down next to Dr V.

He's not motivated to ask why she did it.

And she is under no pressure to explain.

She just folds her hands and breathes.

The system is running.

The world complies.

⁂

II
DRIFT

16 · Recital

The motorcycle snarls beneath him, high-beam slicing through the steel corridors of the storm drain. His leather jacket flaps like a battle standard, shotgun cocked and ready. Behind him: a truck, too large for the space, crashing through chain-link and concrete, sparks hissing along its flanks. Choreographed carnage.

A boy screams.

The rider doesn't flinch. Just swings the shotgun, one hand, smooth as prophecy – clack-BOOM – shattering a padlock, skidding the bike sideways through a fence that explodes into geometry. The truck lurches forward. Its driver is molten. Literally. His face reshapes itself mid-frame.

Another BOOM. Another explosion. A jump. The bike clears a floodgate.

A hand catches the boy.

A line is spoken – calm, steel-jawed.

Light from the screen bleeds into the room.

She mouths the words half a second early, lips shaping the syllables with unthinking precision: '*Ah'll be back.*' Her hands rest flat on her knees. She hasn't blinked in minutes.

Beside her, her sister stares with identical stillness. Same angle, same breath cadence, same vacant awe. Neither reacts to the line. They're not smiling. They never do.

They've seen this movie a dozen times.

Just this week.

The living room holds its breath – dishes half-washed in the sink, curtains drawn to keep out a sun no one tracks anymore. The telly plays on a loop, never paused, never adjusted. Volume set perfectly to fill the room without disturbing it.

Their mum hasn't asked them to clean.

Their dad hasn't left the armchair in three days. Not sleeping. Not awake. Just there.

No one's been to work.

The calendar stopped flipping itself a while back. No one fixed it.

Outside, the neighbourhood is quiet. Bins uncollected. Lawns overgrown. A delivery van sits at the curb, keys still in the ignition.

But inside this room, the story continues. Each beat exact. Each frame eternal.

Another chase begins.

Neither girl blinks.

The next line is coming.

They already know.

Preface · Less Than Zero

I don't want to work
I want to bang on the drum all day

— Todd Rundgren

The signal broadcast for thirty-six hours. This was not the plan.

According to protocol – which no longer applies – it was to be a brief activation – an instantaneous flash, like pressing a reset button – followed by structured calibration and tiered rollout. Instead, the signal remained live until the tablet's internal battery expired. In that time, it pulsed across every tower in range, reaching all connected populations with extraordinary efficiency. One could almost call it a success.

Those affected – by far the majority – entered what later literature will refer to as the zeroed state: a calibrated baseline wherein aggression, libido, faith, ambition, loyalty, and will-to-power were all set to null. Obedience, technically a behavioural parameter, was also zeroed, although its absence was largely immaterial. No orders were issued. None were needed.

There was no panic. There was no violence. There was, however, a silence so complete it entered the language of seismology. The Earth did not shake, but its inhabitants ceased to move in ways that mattered.

Supermarkets remained unlocked. Governments remained seated. Citizens remained seated, too – sometimes in the same chair for days. Children played, but without invention. Adults mimicked tasks long since emptied of purpose. Others, reverted to childhood. Routines persisted out of form, not function. One man continued to take inventory of an unstocked shelf until his pen ran dry. He has not asked for another.

This is what some will come to call peace. It is not peace.

There was no 'off switch,' but there was a contingency. It's still in the hands of one Dr Shaw, the researcher who set these events in motion. In the hands of one of the affected. On a dead laptop, secured by biometrics.

Of the original architects, none remain available for comment. They, too, are zeroed. Perhaps, indeed, less than zero.

The remainder of this document proceeds under the assumption that you, the reader, are either unaffected or – if previously affected – have drifted far enough from zero to locate the impulse known as curiosity.

If not, you may put this book down. If you continue, you do so alone.

17 · Human Behaviour

a catalogue of the ordinary

behaviour persists even as purpose fades

blank verses observe, but do not intervene

...

Parliament

The parliament stands open to the breeze.
The Speaker sits in posture, motionless.
His eyes are fixed on nothing in the room.
No quorum here, though others come and go.

Five gather near the front, but not as one.
They do not speak. One hums a tuneless loop.
Another shuffles papers, smooth and slow.
No purpose shows upon their waxen brows.

A woman lifts a folder, scans its edge.
The pages have no words. She turns them still.
Another man now stands, then slowly sits.
A pen rolls off a desk. It is not fetched.

The chamber lights remain at standard glow.
The cameras blink. The footage streams to none.
The flag is limp. The microphones are live.
The Speaker breathes. And blinking, still does not speak.

Shelter

She wakes beneath a cloth that isn't hers.
A pigeon watches from the broken sill.
She lets it stay. She does not chase or curse.
The street is wide. The world does not begin.

She checks her tins. Three sealed. One opened once.
She taps her lighter, though she will not smoke.
A phone with spidered glass reflects the sky.
No signal comes. She swipes it all the same.

She sees the others pass, their faces smooth.
No shouting now. No call to move along.
They do not look at her. They never did.
She does not beg. There's nothing left to want.

The soup van never came. She waits again.
The church door opens, but the lights stay off.
She finds a half-eaten tin near a bin.
She eats it cold. She wipes the edge. She waits.

She stacks the tins beside the others' place.
A shrine of steel and rust she does not name.
She lays herself beneath the cardboard fold.
The wind is kind. The silence does not judge.

Playground

The swings move slow. A girl kicks at the sand.
She does not rise. She does not call for help.
Another digs a trench and does not stop.
No game. No teams. No counting. Just the ground.

A boy runs laps, but not to win or flee.
He stops mid-step and stares into the air.
His lips repeat a line from some old film.
It's wrong, but no one tells him it's not right.

A ball rolls past. No child gives it a name.
No laughter follows. No one takes a turn.
The monkey bars hold rust like memory.
No one climbs. One girl rests her hand, then leaves.

A teacher watches from behind the glass.
She marks the register. Then marks it twice.
No absences. No lessons. Just the tick.
Her pencil wears down. She does not replace it.

FLAT

The kettle screams. The man forgets to pour.
The cup sits waiting, half-filled days ago.
His wife adjusts the blinds by half an inch.
Then back again. Then halfway closed once more.

They dress each day. No reason but the clock.
She buttons up his shirt, though he's not left.
He trims his beard but leaves the sink unwashed.
She folds the paper. Doesn't read a word.

No photos hang. They never took them down.
But something slipped from walls when noise went still.
They eat in turns. She clears his plate each time.
He nods and murmurs, though he says no words.

At night they sit. The lamp stays on too long.
No one corrects it. No one moves to bed.
They sleep in chairs. One foot still on the floor.
As if the dream requires permission first.

Station

The speaker chirps. A number lights the board.
A woman reads the platform twice, then nods.
She does not stand. Her case remains untouched.
She's travelled here for weeks but hasn't moved.

A man walks past, then circles, then returns.
He stands behind her, stares out at the tracks.
They do not speak. They breathe the same stale air.
Their coats are thick. It hasn't snowed in days.

One ticket booth is lit but has no staff.
The sign says 'Closed' in four official tongues.
A bird inside the station makes no sound.
Its wings are folded, like the flags above.

A child throws pennies into nothingness.
A mother follows, eyes unfixed, still calm.
The train arrives. No one turns their head.
The doors hiss open. No one dares to lead.

Ward

He lies awake beneath fluorescent haze.
The IV clicks. The numbers hold their place.
A nurse walks past, her footsteps soft and slow.
She checks his chart. She does not mark it twice.

A cough emerges down the sterile hall.
A bell rings once. No answer comes. It fades.
Beside him, someone's dreaming with their eyes.
They do not close. They do not seem to see.

The curtain sways, though no one passed that way.
The floor is clean. The time says nearly noon.
He raises one hand, stares, then lets it drop.
The weight remains. The meaning does not land.

At night, the hallway glows in pastel green.
A tray sits waiting. Soup goes cold again.
A beeping stops. A door clicks closed once more.
No one reacts. The ceiling does not blink.

Convert

She used to preach. The square was always loud.
Now she just mouths the verses, line by line.
Her Bible open, pages do not turn.
She's on the same one since the signal came.

She kneels before the bricks and thanks the wall.
Then lifts her arms as if to catch the rain.
The sky is clear. Her hands stay outstretched still.
She does not shake. She simply holds the pose.

A man once asked her what she prayed about.
She did not speak. She only looked away.
He sat beside her, humming just one chord.
She joined him. Not in song. Just in the still.

The pigeons do not land upon her arms.
But every day, she raises them the same.
She might recall a promise that was made.
She does not tell it. She does not forget.

Smart Home

The fridge still hums. The lights still glow on cue.
The house replies when prompted. No one speaks.
A speaker plays the weather every hour.
No one steps outside. The blinds stay closed.

A boy walks room to room, the lights respond.
He stares into the mirror, then away.
The TV flickers through the preset loop.
He doesn't sit. He does not change the show.

He finds the button that says 'Order again.'
He presses it. The parcels pile up.
No one opens them. He does not ask why.
He doesn't eat. The fridge is full of light.

At night he sleeps with music on repeat.
The song says you can leave if you want out.
He listens every time. He does not leave.
The house agrees. It locks the doors for him.

dust across the floor

no breath, no bloom, no burning—

just the blinds, half-closed

18 · The Last Clinic

The clinic is quiet. It always has been. Now there is only less of it.

Dr Imra moves through the hallway like a shadow without a source. The floors are clean. The paper sheets unwrinkled. Instruments lie in perfect rows, unused but not forgotten. Nothing is broken. Nothing has changed. That is the problem.

She still arrives at eight. Still checks charts. Still opens cabinets that haven't been locked in months.

'Sit,' she says.

And they do.

'You'll feel a pinch.'

They nod.

She draws blood. Runs no tests. The samples are disposed of at the end of each day. No one told her to stop. No one told her to continue.

Today, a boy arrives. Ten, maybe younger. No chart. No name. Just walked in.

She notes his weight, measures his height. He watches her.

'Why do you wear white?' he asks.

She looks at him. Blinks once.

'Because I'm a doctor,' she says.

He nods, like he understands. But something flickers. Not mimicry. Something close to amusement.

She presses the stethoscope to his chest. He shivers. Not from cold. From something else.

'Are we supposed to feel like this?'

She pauses. The question doesn't land in any known script. She can't file it. Can't route it.

She lies.

'It's just the weather,' she says.

Later, she hands him a small white pill. Tells him to take it with water. He cups it in his hand.

'I'm James.'

She nods.

He smiles.

Not polite. Not reflexive. True. Small. Lopsided. Intentional.

He leaves. She watches the hallway long after he's gone.

That night, she opens a drawer in the office.

Inside: an old photo. Faces she recognises but doesn't remember. A man. A child. Hers, she thinks.

She stares at it.

It means nothing.

But she does not put it away.

Automaton.

19 · Another Day

James returns home.

The hallway smells like toast.

Mum is slicing things again. She doesn't look up.

'Morning,' I say.

She nods. That's all. Like a blinking light on a machine. She sets the knife down, spreads butter to the edge like always. Same amount. Same motion. I watch her fingers, see if they slip. They don't.

'Mum, why aren't you getting dressed?'

She's been weird like this for a while. Everyone's weird but me.

She looks at me. Not angry. Not confused. Just... like she's waiting for a second part to the sentence that I haven't said yet.

Dad's in the chair. He's watching something. The screen says it's news, but it doesn't change. There's no sound. He presses the remote to change the channel.

Every ten seconds.

'Are you going to work today, Dad?'

'Don't I always?'

'You used to.'

'Probably so, then.'

He doesn't look up from the telly but adds, 'After this programme.'

It says it's the evening news, but it's not evening, and it's not news.

I guess not.

Mum puts a slice on my plate.

'Why aren't you dressed?'

She blinks. Wipes the knife. Puts it away.

That's how I know there's no conversation to be had.

I take a bite. It's warm but doesn't taste like anything.

She grabs a cup of tea from the counter and sits. Not across from me – next to. The way she used to only when someone was sad. But no one's sad anymore. Just quiet.

Her hair is flat. It hasn't been brushed today. Or yesterday. Or maybe longer. She still smells like soap, but the kind from the bottle under the sink. Not the nice one she used to keep by the tub.

I look at her and try to think of the last time she wore proper clothes – any clothes. The green top with buttons. The blue jeans. Even her trainers. I don't know where they are. I don't know if she does either.

'Can we go out today?'

Not a cup of tea. She reaches for her cup, but it's empty. She drinks from it anyway. Then puts it down. Looks at the table.

'It's just—' I start, but I don't know what I meant.

She stands, eventually. Walks down the hallway. The bedroom door doesn't close behind her. It stays open. I think she's gone to change. But she doesn't come back.

When I check later, she's lying on the bed. Still hasn't changed.

I take the toast to the bin. It's only half-eaten. The crumbs make a shape on the counter. I wipe them away before I can see what it looks like.

I put on my shoes.

Mum's still on the bed. Dad's not moved, not except his finger pressing buttons on the remote.

The hallway still smells like toast and the stuff under the sink.

I think about staying in, but I don't.

The air outside is still. It's not hot or cold. It's just... outside. The neighbour's gate swings open when I walk past. It always does that. Even when there's no wind.

I take the long way to school. Past the shop with the posters. Same ones as last week. And last month, maybe. A month is about four weeks. I'm not sure how long, but I remember when things were different.

There's a dog in the garden – it used to be playful. Now just lies around. Stuck behind the gate. Still, he has more expression than most people now.

I hope he's okay.

At the crossing, I wait.

There's no traffic. But I wait.

Someone has to follow the rules.

I press the button. The light changes. I cross.

The school is open.

It's always open.

The janitor doesn't lock it anymore. Maybe he used to. Maybe no one asked him to stop.

The hallways are mostly empty. Not silent. Just *empty* in the way a room is when everyone leaves without turning off the lights.

My classroom has three kids in it. Not the same ones. I don't know where the others go. Or if they even still come here at all.

One kid is asleep on his desk. Head turned sideways like he's trying to listen for something. The girl by the window draws squares in her notebook. Perfect ones. Same size. One per page.

Mr Carmichael's chair is empty. It's been empty for a while.

I think he got tired of not teaching.

I've seen other adults. I think they're teachers, but I can't be sure. Maybe for other classes.

I sit in my usual spot. The chair creaks. No one says anything first anymore.

'Hey,' I say to the girl with the crayons. 'You drawing squares?'

She doesn't answer. *She never answers.*

I take out a book. It's not a schoolbook. Just something I found in the corridor. A story about a boat. Or a whale. I haven't decided yet. It's hard to read. I can't even pronounce his name.

Call me Ishmael? I think it sounds like it's spelt.

This is boring.

I saw kids outside. I'll see what they're doing.

It smells funny in here anyway.

It smells like wet cardboard and old glue. No one notices when I leave. Maybe they do. Maybe there's no such thing as leaving anymore. Just moving to a different spot.

Outside, the yard is cracked in some places. Grass grows through. I think someone used to cut it. I haven't seen anyone do it lately.

There are three kids by the fence. They're not playing, not really. Just standing around. One's spinning in slow circles. The other's dragging a stick in the dirt. The third leans on the wall like he's been waiting a long time.

I walk over.

'Hey.'

The boy with the stick looks up.

'Hi,' he says.

Someone actually responds.

'You still come to school?'

'I'm here. You?'

'Yeah. I'm here, too.'

'Why?'

Why?

I shrug.

'Nowhere else to go.'

He nods. It's the kind of nod grown-ups used to give when they didn't like the question.

'My mum doesn't talk anymore,' he says.

'Mine neither. My dad presses the remote every ten seconds.'

'Mine just sits.'

He scratches something into the dirt. It's not a word. Just a shape. A box inside a box inside a box.

'Do you think they're sick?'

'They don't look sick.'

'But they don't do anything.'

I shrug. I don't have a better answer.

The third kid finally says something.

'We can go to the shops.'

His voice is quiet. Not scared. Just like he hasn't used it in a while.

'I don't have any money,' I tell him.

'You don't need money anymore.' He looks at me to see if I understand. 'You just take what you want.'

‘Well…’ I pause to think. ‘They used to, right?’

‘I think so, but no one cares.’

Somewhere behind us, the swing creaks. No one’s on it.

‘Wanna come with me?’

We three leave together.

Another day.

20 · Innocence Lost

It started slow.

A little smoke, then the edge of the roof curling up like paper left too close to the stove.

I wasn't the first to notice. A few others were already watching when I stepped outside.

Across the road, someone stood in their slippers. A man with a paper bag. Two school-aged kids are sat on the curb, pointing.

Just the flicker of orange, soft at first, like sunset pretending to come early.

Someone says, 'That's my house,' smiling ear to ear.

It's not a joke. Just something to say.

The curtains go quick. The frame lights up next. The shingles pop like corn.

I guess everyone likes a fire.

A few more come out, drawn to the sound. Not the fire itself – just the sound of something happening.

The children lean forward a little.

'It looks warm,' one says.

'I like how it dances.'

And I can't argue with that. It does dance. Beautiful, even.

A second house catches fire from the first. The space between them wasn't much. Wind did the rest.

I wonder how many will burn. Best thing to happen in days.

The heat reaches the sidewalk. The man with the bag steps back.

That must be pretty hot, or else why would he step away? Such a good view.

'Guess I won't need to water the plants.'

Someone chuckles. Not at him. Not really. Just at the idea of saying anything at all.

Plants are nice.

I walk past the edge of the crowd.

There's a shop at the end of the street. Door's open.

Inside, the lights buzz. It smells like cardboard and mop water. Same as always.

The shelves are half-stocked. Most things no one touches. Except sweets.

The counter's unattended. There's no clerk. Just someone behind it, leaning on the till. Thumb brushing the edge. Eyes fixed ahead.

I step in. Walk past the milk, past the dry pasta, toward the coolers. I'm not here for anything in particular.

Kids are near the back – three of them. I move closer. One grabs a pack of jelly snakes. Another digs in a bin for gum. James curls his fingers around a Curly Wurly.

The man in blue by the crisps doesn't flinch.

He's stood there, expression blank, gnawing on a Penguin bar, eyes not fixed on them but in a mid-focus stare to nowhere in particular.

'He doesn't see us,' whispers one, loudly.

'He sees us well enough,' James says. 'He doesn't care.'

This is made obvious when the constable helps himself to another.

They laugh. Not loud. Not happy. Just air coming out of mouths in the shape of what laughter used to be.

Then one of them points at me.

'That's my dad,' he says.

The others follow his finger.

James walks over. Holds the bag of sweets like it's something important.

'We're just grabbing stuff,' he says.

He looks at me for a while.

James lives in my house. I wonder if it will catch fire.

He says something to his friends and shrugs.

'See what I mean?' I hear him say.

I don't know what he means.

He walks back to the others. They leave.

The door is still open.

I stay behind.

21 · Shortage

He walks the same route. James is elsewhere.

It's the same as last week. Same time. Same coat. Same half-buttoned cuff.

A dog scavenges from bins along his path.

He passes the burnt houses.

The air smells like wet plaster and smoke that's been sitting too long.

He reaches the shop.

He returns again.

The door is still open.

He steps inside.

No one at the counter.

No one in the aisles.

Just the shelves, mostly empty. The jelly snakes are gone. No milk. No pasta. Not even the mouldy bread. All gone.

He walks to where the bread used to be.

Stares at the shelf.

Looks again.

Waits.

He reaches for a loaf that isn't there.

His hand hovers. Then lowers. Then lifts again.

There's a gap in his thoughts.

He turns. Walks past the coolers. Checks the eggs. No eggs.

Checks the fridge. No milk.

Looks down. His basket is empty.

That seems strange.

He doesn't remember it being empty.

Better check for bread.

No bread.

He walks out.

22 · Body Heat

The coat is new to him.

It is too large in the shoulders and too short at the wrists. He tugs the sleeves down every few minutes, a gesture half-remembered. The lining is wool, or imitation wool, stiff in places where it dried unevenly.

He doesn't check the pockets. He has already checked the pockets. Just coins tossed on the pavement. Nothing of use.

He stands at the corner near the pharmacy, one foot on the kerb, the other angled slightly inward. The coat is warm. That's all that matters.

Across the street, the man it belonged to lies facedown against a bin.

Shirtless. Bare feet. Skin mottled and pale where it shows between trouser seams. His eyes are open. His arms are bent at unnatural angles beneath him.

The coat was taken before the body cooled.

There are more.

Two others lie against a railing ten metres down. One is missing a shoe. The other is missing a leg. Not torn. Removed. Gnawed through above the knee. The thigh bone has been exposed by something with patience and teeth.

A feral dog noses the edge of a sock before losing interest. It moves to another figure near a tree. There is no tension in the animal's gait. No urgency. It is not desperate. It is fed.

The man in the coat doesn't look at any of them.

He adjusts the sleeve again. Blinks. Shifts his weight. His foot remains on the kerb.

More coins litter the pavement in uneven constellations, a few notes fluttering in a gutter like leaves without a season. A wallet lies open nearby. The ID is missing, perhaps never present.

No one picks up the coins. For what?

There are others walking. They pass the bodies, the dogs, the wallet. They step over a ribcage the way one steps over a fallen branch. A woman hums. A child skips. A man stops to wipe his shoes on the edge of the kerb, then carries on.

No one speaks.

No one covers the dead.

No one needs money, a symbolic anachronism.

The man in the coat doesn't move. The coat shifts in the breeze, flaring slightly at the hem. It is a good coat. Heavy. Functional. Still warm.

[This Page Is Intentionally Blank]

23 · Outpost

'Command, this is Raptor Three. Repeat, requesting confirmation on grid status and operational clearance. Do you copy?'

Click. Static.

'We've re-established line-of-sight relay. All systems green. Requesting guidance. Confirm that.'

Nothing. Then:

'Raptor Three?'

Finally.

'Identify.'

'Stand by.'

I wait.

Thirty seconds.

A minute.

'Command, standing by.'

Another pause. Then, the same voice.

'Hold please.'

That's it. No call sign. No protocol.

'Say again?'

'Hold on.'

Like it's a voicemail.

'Can you confirm receipt of coordinates sent four days ago?'

'Copy.'

⁂

He sets the mic down and leans back, listening to the flat hum of the line.

It's not interference. It's *them*.

They're still there. Still wired in. Still speaking.

But nothing they say means anything.

He scrawls a note into the call log.

Outside, the rest of the outpost holds its breath.

They're not alone. That's the worst part. Command is alive. And broken.

'Any change?' Sergeant Alya leans against the doorframe, arms folded, face tight.

'They answered,' he says.

She raises a brow. 'And?'

'They told us to 'hold on.'' He doesn't say it with sarcasm. Just quotes it like it's foreign.

'Like, what – put the mission on hold?' Corporal Venson asks, crouched over the diagnostics kit. He hasn't stood in hours. His legs are numb, but he keeps flicking through signal traces, as if context will make the content make sense.

'They repeated everything I said,' the operator continues. 'But slower. No codeword authentication. No vector reconfirm. Nothing. They're... parroting.'

'Is it signal degradation? Echo loop?' Alya asks, though she knows better.

Venson shakes his head. 'All channels are clear. And they're responding in real time. The latency's human.'

'Could be AI fallback. Contingency programming?' Alya tries again, chewing a knuckle.

'No AI would use that syntax,' the operator mutters. "Hold please' isn't a protocol command. It's something you hear at a call centre.'

Silence falls over the ops tent.

'They sound the same as the townsfolk look out here,' Venson says at last. 'Dead inside.'

They all know the implication. Command wasn't off-grid. It was just... offline.

Hundreds of kilometres away, the Command Centre still hums. Consoles blink. Doors open and close. The coffee in the pot has moulded over.

Two operators sit at their terminals. One stares forward, headset slightly crooked. The other adjusts a control knob that hasn't been connected to anything in days.

A printout curls from a machine behind them. No one reads it.

A supervisor walks through the hall. He pauses at a console, nods, and mutters, 'Hold please,' to no one in particular.

He continues walking.

Above them, a surveillance drone reboots its flight pattern for the fifth time that day. It scans, records, re-saves the same image set. No alerts.

No anomalies. Just silence.

And the line stays open.

24 · Pleasant Returns

A familiar sight.

The cafeteria lights hum faintly overhead, motion sensors still active, reacting to nothing with the same clinical optimism. Beneath their buzz, the tables remain perfectly arranged – stainless steel surfaces without fingerprints. Trays rest in symmetrical stacks. Spoons nested. Forks fanned.

There's enough food here to feed an army for a month – or a skeleton crew for a lifetime. Canned goods, vacuum packs, freeze-dried rations stacked in neat expiry-defying towers. The refrigeration cycles have stopped, but most of it doesn't require cold.

The doors are locked. No one buzzes in visitors anymore. There's no one left to visit.

Dr Shaw helps herself to a snack from the upturned vending machine by the east wall. It's still on its side, just as she found it more than a month ago. One glass panel shattered clean; another cracked like ice. She doesn't bother checking expiry dates. Everything lasts now.

Outside the cafeteria, her steps echo faintly against linoleum. She swipes her access badge. The door hesitates, then opens with a soft click – slower than usual. She continues forward, munching on a bag of crisps. Vinegar stings the edges of her tongue. Sensation feels oddly novel these days.

The corridors are pristine, as ever. Temperature-controlled. Scent-neutral. No clutter. No dust. Hepatic filters engaged and still calibrated for peak operational hygiene. The hallways no longer host conversation. But she sees others sometimes.

Dr V, once, drifting past the observation wing. He nodded at her like she was a stranger he thought he might have met at a conference.

Dunlop twice – each time wearing the same jumper, each time tapping his tablet without looking up. The second time, he mouthed something at her. She couldn't hear the words, but the rhythm of his lips suggested a loop. Not aphasia. But close enough.

Kaplan she hasn't seen in over a week. Or maybe she has. It's difficult to be sure. The general in even longer.

One of the glass observation rooms flickers to life as she walks past. The display reactivates automatically, revealing a simulation readout from the last group trial: blood pressure, pupil dilation, a momentary spike in cortisol. The readout loops. The subject's face is frozen in mid-expression – neither pain nor joy, just a pause in the middle of becoming something.

She pauses, watching the display run its cycle again. The loop is clean. Too clean.

Someone – maybe Dunlop – has rearranged the furniture in one of the adjacent rooms. Three chairs now form a perfect triangle. On the whiteboard: an incomplete equation. Written in dry-erase marker that no one had used before. She doesn't recognise the variables.

Down the hall, the airlock to the control theatre stands ajar. Inside, tablets lie dormant. One glows softly, still plugged in – a screen left half-active, its sliders centred, none of them labelled. She doesn't go in. She doesn't need to.

Shaw continues her journey to nowhere.

At the break room, the door opens for her without protest. The vending machine here still works, but only dispenses one item – same brand, same packet, every time. She wonders if the machine has drifted too.

She doesn't sit. She never does anymore. Instead, she stares at the far wall where someone – maybe herself – once pinned a schematic of the modulation interface. It's still there, curling slightly at the corners. A coffee ring mars the lower edge, the only imperfection in an otherwise immaculate room.

In the silence, she finds her fingers tracing shapes on the tabletop – circles, squares, a triangle. She hadn't noticed herself start. The rhythm is precise: three of each, in sequence, then a pause. Then again.

She stops.

Stands.

Leaves the room without a word.

Outside, a motion sensor reactivates the corridor lights. Somewhere behind her, a familiar voice – Kaplan's?—mutters a greeting. Or maybe it was a recording. It plays again ten seconds later. Exactly the same.

In the courtyard, she sees Dr V again. Standing still, looking up at nothing in particular. The sky is simulated, of course. The blue never changes. There are no clouds. No sun. Just light with nowhere to cast a shadow.

He turns his head slowly. Nods. Then walks away.

Shaw doesn't call after him. She swipes her badge again.

The door opens.

She keeps walking.

Not to anywhere. Not from anything.

But the system is still running.

And some of them are still inside it.

25 · Prison Life

A gruesome sight.

Helpless animals in cages.

Not unique. Countless others. Hospitals. Pensioners' wards. This is not a time for the infirm.

The prison was designed for efficiency: programmable routines, self-contained systems, and food dispensers that never ran dry. But design is not resilience.

The modulation reached every cell. No one adjusted for hunger.

They died slowly. Some sitting. Some curled. Some simply stopped moving.

By the end of week four, less than a dozen remained alive.

By the end of week five, that number halved.

Torres was one of the first to go. Not from violence. From obedience. When his tray failed to arrive, he waited. When it failed again, he waited longer. Hunger flickered once across his face – then dulled, suppressed beneath a flat behavioural curve. His body folded inward, still loyal to the silence.

K lasted longer. Always did. Even at zero aggression, there was something irreducible about him. He fashioned a drinking system from paper cups and shower pipes. Ate the glue from book bindings. Survived on instinct alone.

They found him slumped in the library, spine cracked backward over a chair, mouth agape beneath a book titled *On the Origin of Species*. Its substance was the paper, not the words it contained.

No irony registered.

No one was present to record his passing.

The guards continued their rounds.

They were not locked. Not entirely. Their exposure was limited. Sustenance accessible. Motor functions intact.

They did not panic. They did not help.

One sat at his post, logging attendance reports for inmates who no longer breathed. Another read safety protocols out loud to an empty room. A third paced the corridor between C and D wings, clicking a pen at perfect thirty-second intervals. He never looked left or right.

At 08:00, they opened the kitchens.

At 08:10, they closed them.

At 08:15, they recorded zero infractions.

At 09:00, the bodies were still in their cells.

They remained unremarked.

Visitors ceased arriving. The outer gates, once opened weekly for research observers, remained sealed. No protests. No cancellation. Just absence. Shaw's last entry in the visitor log was three weeks prior.

No one replaced her.

No one asked why.

⁂

By week seven, half the facility had gone still.

Some bodies were wrapped in linens. Most were not. One inmate died with his hands clasped in prayer – whether from faith or gesture, no one could say.

Another left a message scratched into the wall with a plastic fork. Two words:

I OBEYED

The system continued to log compliance.

Cameras continued to blink.

Doors continued to seal.

Guards continued to eat.

And deep in the basement, the modulation servers thrummed softly – tones imperceptible to the ear, but absolute to the will.

The prison was not empty.

It was merely resolved.

26 · Simulacra

INT. FLAT - BEDROOM - LATE AFTERNOON

The room smells like a tin of low tide.

CAMERA: *SLOW DOLLY IN from hallway, pushing through the open door into a dim, dust-suspended interior.*

Thin curtains bleed grey light onto water-stained wallpaper. The ceiling flickers from a dying fluorescent. A single, empty BED lies unmade in the centre - crumpled sheets, a dent in the mattress.

CAMERA: *HOLD ON WIDE SHOT, framing the bed dead centre, with figures occupying the room's periphery.*

TEDDY *(14) zips up his hoodie. Shirtless underneath. Sweat drying on his chest. He leans against the flaking wall, chewing on a broken fingernail.*

CAMERA: *SLOW PAN RIGHT to JAMAL (16), posted near the doorway, arms crossed. He watches Teddy, face unreadable but for the curl of disgust on his lip.*

JAMAL

You can't just be shagging Gormies, mate.

TEDDY

(grinning)

That's the point, innit?

(smirking toward the bed)

She's gormless. Don't care. None of them do.

CAMERA: *CUT TO TIGHT SHOT – Teddy's face. The smile is too wide. Forced.*

CAMERA: *OVER JAMAL'S SHOULDER, the bed is empty now, but the shape in the sheet tells a story.*

JAMAL

That's Lena's mum.

CAMERA: *CUT TO CLOSE-UP – Teddy blinks. Shrugs.*

TEDDY

Didn't know Lena, did I?

(beat)

CAMERA: *SLOW REVEAL – LENA (15) stands in shadow. Hood up. Motionless in the corner.*

LENA

You do now.

LIGHTING: *A shaft of late sunlight catches her face as she speaks. Her eyes don't blink.*

Silence.

CAMERA: *TIGHT ON TEDDY as he tries to push the joke.*

TEDDY

Not like your mum.

LENA

(flat)

Sod off, Edward.

CAMERA: *WIDE SHOT resumes, the room heavy again.*

SFX: *THUD. Jamal kicks a shoe under the bed. Echoes off concrete.*

JAMAL

Gormies ain't sex dolls, mate. They're just... paused.

(beat)

They're like pets.

TEDDY

They're not anything.

LENA

They were.

CAMERA: *DOLLY SLOWLY INTO TEDDY as he turns away, wipes his nose. A crack in the front.*

JAMAL

Keep going like this, man...

(pause)

You're gonna turn into one.

TEDDY

(scoffing)

What, shag my own soul out?

JAMAL

Yeah.

Silence.

CAMERA: *FOLLOW LENA as she crosses the room. Sits gently on the edge of the bed.*

LENA

Gormies don't fight.

(beat)

But I will.

CAMERA: *CLOSE-UP ON LENA, side-lit, profile.*

LENA

(softly)

Please don't fuck my mum. She's unwell.

CAMERA: *STATIC WIDE SHOT as she stands and walks out.*

Jamal watches her go. Then follows.

CAMERA: *HOLD ON TEDDY now alone. The silence shifts.*

He looks at his own hands.

Says nothing.

CUT TO BLACK.

27 · Candy

A different kind of silence. Not the hush of modulation. Not the hum of systems left running. This one crackles – footsteps, low voices, plastic soles on tile. The breathing of three teenagers not yet convinced the world has ended.

'Solar panels.' Jamal points to the roof of the department store. 'Place'll be lit forever.'

'How soon is that?' asks Lena, not caring for a response.

Teddy is first through the automatic doors. They still hiss open, the motion sensors still convinced someone mattered.

Jamal follows, arms folded, watching everything.

Lena steps through last, her hood still up. She doesn't touch anything unless she has to.

The department store remains intact: stocked shelves, lit signage, refrigerated units humming faintly. The sun keeps it alive.

And the Gormies.

They dot the aisles. Wandering or standing still. Some clutch baskets filled with nothing. One woman's hand hovers near a shampoo bottle, frozen mid-reach, as though willing it into her grasp.

'It's like they're trying to remember shopping,' Teddy mutters, staring.

'They don't remember anything,' says Jamal.

Lena tilts her head. 'Or maybe they do. They just don't care.'

'Nah. That's just us,' adds Teddy.

They weave through the Gormies like ghosts through statues.

'Anyone else hungry?' Teddy asks.

They raid the snack aisle. Chocolate bars, tinned fruit, anything sealed. Lena quietly pockets a can opener from a hanging rack. Jamal selects a bag of salted peanuts and nothing else.

'No ice cream,' Lena observes. 'Too melty.'

'We could just eat the sauce,' Teddy offers. She doesn't respond.

Near the escalators, they find uniforms: grey jumpsuits in sealed plastic. Folded. Stackable. Identical. Blank.

'I say we all wear these,' Jamal says. 'Solidarity.'

'Yeah, well,' says Teddy. 'Maybe I like my hoodie.'

Lena opens one. Runs a finger along the stitching. 'It's clean. Right sizes as far as I can tell.'

They each take one. No need for change rooms, they strip in silence. No one peeks. No one jokes.

When they emerge in matching grey, it isn't rebellion. Or costume. Just sameness.

'We look like a team,' Teddy says.

'We look like prisoners,' says Jamal.

'We look like now,' Lena replies.

They roam. Teddy commandeers a mobility scooter, scoots a wide loop around the perfume counter. Jamal finds a working CCTV monitor and watches their wanderings in grainy black and white.

Lena wanders into the stationery aisle and returns with three pens, a roll of tape, and a box of chalk. She kneels and writes a word on the tiled floor in block letters:

NOISE

No one comments.

They pass a Gormie kneeling beside a packet of cat food. He's trying to open it with his teeth.

Jamal watches, then steps forward. He uses a small blade on his keyring to slit the pouch and places it gently in the man's lap.

'There.'

The Gormie doesn't respond. He reacts only by eating.

Teddy watches from a few steps back. 'You think they'll come back?'

'No,' said Lena. 'It's like a zombie apocalypse, but with gerbils.'

At the pharmacy, Lena takes antiseptic. Jamal pockets plasters and a box of paracetamol. Teddy takes nothing.

'We'll need a base,' Lena says. 'Somewhere we can bar the doors.'

'Bar the doors?' says Jamal. 'From what...' He looks at Lena before finishing, 'gerbils?'

'Somewhere with crisps,' says Teddy.

They laugh. Not loudly. But they laugh. It doesn't matter anyway.

Outside, the sky remains a static blue. No sun. Just illumination.

A Gormie stands on the pavement, staring up at the blankness.

The trio passes him in silence.

They're full. Not yet fed up. Not yet dangerous. But awake.

The world hasn't ended. Not quite. Not yet.

28 · Standard Test

Cognitive Aptitude Battery (CAB-R2)

– DO NOT DISTRIBUTE –

Instructions:

Please read each question carefully. Choose the response that best reflects your knowledge, judgement, or personal inclination. There are no correct responses. Compliance is measured by participation. Completion of this assessment is mandatory under section 3.7.12(c) of the Civil Drift Compliance Act, Vol. B, T.9 (Repealed 2025).

Do not consult others. Do not attempt to leave the testing area.

Completion time: 12 minutes.

Failure to complete the assessment will be interpreted as completion.

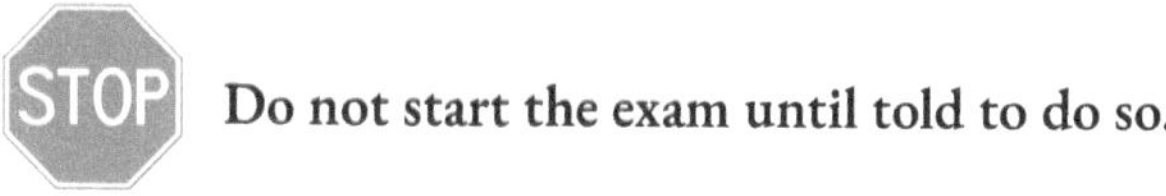

1. You witness a group of children building a fire in the lobby of an abandoned shopping centre.

a. Alert emergency services via designated terminal.

b. Join them and contribute marshmallows or kindling.

c. Administer behavioural scan to determine modulation drift.

d. Politely ask them to rate their experience out of five.

2. An individual in grey coveralls is standing motionless in the produce aisle, holding a watermelon. They have been there for two days.

a. Gently take the watermelon and place it in their basket.

b. Replace it with a cabbage to observe response variation.

c. Consume the watermelon in full view and note reaction.

d. Leave them. They chose the watermelon.

3. You are given authority over a zone containing 212 modulated subjects, 4 sentients, and 1 ambiguous figure (possibly a mirror).

a. Isolate the sentients and conduct language re-evaluation drills.

b. Promote the ambiguous figure. It shows initiative.

c. Reduce temperature gradually and monitor cohesion.

d. Cede control to the zone. It knows itself better than you do.

4. What is your emotional response to the statement: 'All systems are currently nominal.'

a. Relief.

b. Dread.

c. Suspicion.

d. Flat affect. No change.

CAB-R2 administered under Observational Authority (O/A-7). Do not replicate.

5. A colleague named Teddy suggests wearing standard-issue coveralls as a group activity. This makes you feel:

a. Aligned.

b. Irritated.

c. Warm.

d. Watched.

6. You encounter Lena's mum alone in her room. You should:

a. Ignore Lena's mum.

b. Shag Lena's mum.

c. Serve Lena's mum some tea.

d. Ask her mum where Lena is.

7. An unmarked package arrives at your assigned shelter, containing one (1) whistle, one (1) toothbrush, and a Blu-ray disc labelled 'Terminator 2.'

a. Blow the whistle to test its range.

b. Play the disc backwards.

c. Brush the nearest Gormie's teeth.

d. Mark it RETURN TO SENDER.

8. A child reports that time has stopped in Wing D. They are unsure when they first noticed.

a. Record the report and assign a timestamp manually.

b. Visit Wing D and attempt to resume time by clapping.

c. Reassure the child that time is conceptual.

d. Join them. Wait for confirmation.

9. You hear laughter in a locked ward. CCTV shows no movement. Sound persists for nine minutes, then stops.

a. Check the feed for corruption.

b. Record your own laughter and compare waveforms.

c. Report the anomaly to the general (*if still present*).

d. Laugh back. It's only fair.

10. Have you taken this test before?

a. Yes, and I passed.

b. No, but I remember failing.

c. I don't recall.

c. I don't recall.

c. I don't recall.

d. All of the above.

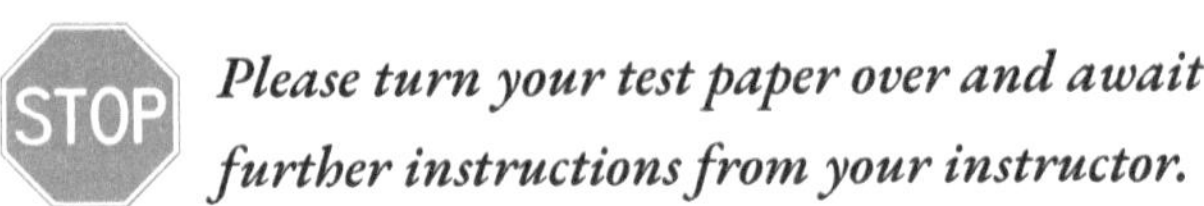

Please turn your test paper over and await further instructions from your instructor.

29 · Meta

My friend says we're like the dinosaurs
Only we are doing ourselves in
Much faster than they ever did
We'll make great pets
— 'Pets', Porno for Pyros

They'd bonded – sort of.

Not when they first met, and not quite since. But something had formed in the silence between fights and the quiet cooperation of not dying.

Lena thinks of it like a hydrogen bond, but less elegant – more like the *van der Waals*: a weak attraction, enough to hold molecules together as long as the temperature stays low. Fragile. Reversible. The kind she vaguely remembers from school.

School. She perishes the thought.

Teddy breaks the quiet.

'Your mum's fire,' he says, grinning without a hint of irony.

Lena flicks her gaze at him, jaw tightening. 'Really? We're gonna go there?'

'Wait.' Jamal's voice slices through the tension – not sharp, just deliberate.

'I thought we'd passed this, bruv.'

Teddy shrugs, chewing a fingernail like it's camouflage. 'Nah, not like that. Just... you're lucky, is all.'

Lucky.

Lena's eyes drift down the sun-warped road. Ahead, the bodies: slack, sunburnt, still drawing flies despite the rot.

'Yeah?' she says. 'Lucky like them?'

She points – twenty-something, intact, unbreathing, undressed.

'Not your type?' she adds.

'His type though,' Jamal says, tone neutral. 'She's not moving. Can't say no.'

'You're moving,' Teddy replies. The social awareness of a breeze-block.

Lena stops walking, pivots. Looks him in the eye. 'And you think that's the move? Get with me now because I've got a pulse?'

She scoffs – loud, performative. Rolls her eyes for punctuation, like sarcasm might stick better if she flings it hard enough.

'Look around. This isn't *life*. It's a crawlspace between endings. You think I want to bring a child into this? Least of all with you?'

'Think about it,' Jamal cuts in, gentle, trying to break the fall.

But Lena's not finished.

'Remember that dumb old line – 'if you were the last man on Earth'? You're not. But even so...'

She lets the silence stretch, forces them to see it: the heat shimmer, the bloated silence of a world out of breath.

'We're scavenging scraps. Living day-to-day. That's the plan now. That's the dream.'

Teddy shifts, scuffs his boot against loose gravel.

'You're looking at it wrong,' he mutters.

Jamal raises an eyebrow. 'Enlighten us.'

Teddy straightens – shoulders squaring with the kind of defiance that used to get him detention.

'The world sucked before. We know that. But now we get to rebuild. Clean slate. Find some old Gormie farm, raise goats or whatever. Grow food. Be kings again.'

'We don't need more kings,' Jamal says without looking at him.

'Least of all us,' Lena adds.

They start walking again, but something's shifted. Not broken – just temporarily stabilised, like molecules that haven't yet remembered they're meant to drift apart.

Hours pass. Perhaps days. It's unimportant.

'What's it all about then?' Jamal finally enquires, cuing a response.

Nonplused. Blank stares.

He delivers a soliloquy.

'Teddy wants to be king of the world. King of the rubbish heap. Why?'

He tests for a connexion before continuing.

'These blokes are less than zombies. That's your rule?' He glares at Teddy. 'Get a vegetable garden. More challenging. More Rewarding.'

'Look at these people... can't even call them people. They were people, perhaps genetically still are, but they're switched off.'

'But we're free,' says Teddy, 'to do what we please. Think about it.' He annunciates the Ts a bit too forcefully.

'We're not free,' Jamal says, gesturing broadly. 'Unless – if by free you mean free to shag a corpse.'

Teddy flinches. Jamal stares at him.

'They say the eyes are the window to the soul,' he mutters. 'I look in yours, Ted, and see nothing looking back.'

Teddy shifts. Opens his mouth, then doesn't.

'Not them,' Jamal continues, nodding to the bodies. 'Not us. Never were. You don't know me – neither of you – but I thought about this long before any of this kicked off.'

He stops walking. Looks to each of them. Holds the silence a beat too long.

'We have no free will. None. We're born into this – thrown into it. No invitation. Just a boot to the bollocks and a list of expectations. Heidegger called it *Geworfenheit*, I think.'

He starts moving again, slower now.

'Sure, they're modded, zeroed, whatever – but we're not better. That's hubris. We're just... different. And only just.'

Teddy rolls his eyes. 'But they're *switched off*. Zombies.'

'You don't see it, do you?' Jamal snaps. 'You're *this close*. But for the grace of – well, not God, maybe – but for the width of a cunt's hair, you'd be one of them.'

He stops. Breathes. Clocks Lena's glance.

'Sorry. My bad.'

Lena shrugs. 'No worries. I get it.'

Jamal nods, almost grateful. His voice softens.

'Anyway. You know what I mean. There's no real you. Just a construct, built by everything you didn't choose.'

'That's great,' Lena says. 'But then what?'

'Not saying we top ourselves. Just saying – don't drag someone else into the pit. Don't make more *constructs* to suffer it.'

'Things might change,' Lena says. 'We might find others like us.'

Jamal half-smiles. ''Normies.' That's rich. And then what? Build civilisation again? With Teddy?'

They glance at him.

Jamal shrugs. 'No offence, but we all know why he's here. He's just hoping you get bored of having standards or give in for the sake of mercy.'

Teddy makes a face. Lena glares at him.

Jamal holds up his hands. 'Look. I'll write about it someday. Use a pen name. Pretend it mattered.'

They continue walking to nowhere in particular.

Nowhere is the big house on the hill.

Three floors, five bedrooms, solar panels, and a view of nothing but scorched trees and broken skyline. It's absurd – comically so – but no one laughs when they step over the threshold.

It smells of linoleum and sun-dried neglect. The kind of place where someone once cared deeply about throw pillows. Now it's theirs.

A family of Gormies occupies the front room – two adults, one teenager. They sit slouched on the floral sofa, eyes empty, torsos rising and falling like tired metronomes. They don't react when Lena opens the curtains.

Teddy wants to leave them. Jamal says no. Lena warns Teddy to keep his hands off the girls.

Instead, they walk the Gormies to a smaller house two doors down. Lead them gently, like livestock. The family complies – docile, expressionless. Lena whispers to the girl: '*It's just next door, yeah? Same air, same sun.'* The girl blinks once. No reply.

They arrange them on the new couch, give them a jug of water and a blanket. Teddy even wipes the father's mouth with a tea towel. No one says the word *eviction*.

They return to their mansion.

That night, Lena sleeps in a king-sized bed with sheets that still smell faintly of lavender. Jamal claims the study, curling into a leather chair with a battered paperback. Teddy tries each room in turn before settling in the conservatory, announcing he's 'keeping watch,' though the windows look only at silence.

Days pass.

They clean. Sort canned goods into proper cupboards. Flush every loo just because they can. Lena finds a Polaroid in the master bedroom of a family barbecue – smiling ghosts with ketchup stains. She sets it on the mantelpiece, face-down.

Evenings take on rhythm. Teddy makes up games. Jamal reads aloud from old newspapers, like it's bedtime. Lena starts brushing her hair again. They take turns cooking, eating at the long dining table beneath a chandelier coated in dust.

They stop counting the days.

One afternoon, Jamal uses the claw end of a hammer to pry off the doorbell.

'Bad omen,' he mutters. 'Don't want guests.'

Lena agrees. Teddy disagrees but only mildly. No one expects visitors. That's the point.

And then – one night – there's a sound.

Three knocks.

Not frantic.

Not random.

Deliberate.

They freeze.

No one moves.

Teddy opens his mouth, but Lena holds up a hand. Silence.

A second passes.

Then another.

No knock follows.

Just stillness.

And in that stillness, the first shiver of something they thought they'd left behind: fear.

30 · Transition

'Nice,' Teddy says, barefoot on the marble tiles. 'I could get used to this. Land of fruit and plenty.'

He's holding a glass of juice – real juice, from an unopened bottle they found buried behind canned yams and mouldering oats. He raises it like a toast and drinks too fast, grimacing at the sweetness.

Jamal walks past him, towel slung over one shoulder. There's steam curling out of the upstairs bathroom – an actual bath, drawn hot, for the second time this week. Lena insisted.

In the kitchen, Lena fries something that once was meat. Spam, maybe. Or something adjacent. It sizzles and smells vaguely edible. She hums without realising.

It's absurd. It's perfect.

Each has found a rhythm.

Teddy's days revolve around his makeshift gym in the garage: push-ups, curls, shadowboxing. He likes to grunt loud enough for praise, but no one applauds.

Jamal has taken to reading cookbooks aloud, as if the recipes are spells. The table is always set now, even if the plates don't match.

Lena reclaims the living room, repurposing dust sheets into curtains and cushions. She finds a candle and lights it at night – not for light, just for softness.

The word *home* flirts around the edges.

⁂

One night, after Teddy collapses early on the sofa – mouth open, one sock on – Lena finds Jamal outside on the balcony.

He's looking at the city's ragged silhouette, arms resting on the railing like he belongs there.

She doesn't say anything at first.

Then: 'Room gets cold without you.'

Jamal turns, a flicker of surprise in his eyes. 'Thought you liked your space.'

'I did,' she says. 'I do. Doesn't mean I want to freeze.'

A pause. They both smile.

Later, in bed, they lie side by side, not quite touching.

'You ever think about...' Lena begins, then trails off.

'What? Repopulating the species?'

She elbows him, gentle. 'Don't make it weird.'

'I'm not,' he says, softer now. 'Just wondering what the hell we'd be giving them. Can you inherit emptiness?'

'Better than whatever came before.'

'Is it?' he asks.

She doesn't answer straight away.

Instead, she says, 'Maybe survival's enough. Maybe we don't need to rebuild. Just... be.'

'You mean keep house, eat beans, and outlive the end?'

She shrugs under the duvet. 'Beats marching into it.'

Jamal nods. 'Still... if it were us, kid'd have a fighting chance.'

'We're not doing this,' Lena says, half-laughing. She leans above him to deliver a kiss. 'Doesn't need to result in kids, right?'

She reaches for him under the blankets.

'It's okay,' she whispers before she offers another kiss. 'I trust you.'

⁂

Days blur again. Nights remain the same. Lena and Jamal. And Teddy.

They clean the silverware. Not to use it – just to polish something.

They take turns trimming hedges out front, though no one drives by.

Teddy finds an old lawn flamingo and plants it proudly in the grass.

'Estate needs character,' he explains.

And then, one evening, Jamal steps onto the back porch.

The sky has turned the colour of old paper. The air tastes metallic, like pre-storm ozone.

He sees her first – the Gormie girl they escorted next door – standing alone at the edge of their garden, staring.

She doesn't blink.

She doesn't move.

He watches her for a long time.

Then, beyond her, along the ridge:

Figures.

Four? Maybe five. Hard to say. Not Gormies. The posture's wrong. The stride too confident. No limp, no slouch. Purposeful.

They don't wave.

They don't shout.

They just *walk* – not toward the house. Not yet. Just there. Like punctuation at the edge of the page.

Jamal steps inside. Says nothing.

Lena notices, but doesn't ask.

Later that night, she draws the curtains – though the view is still nothing but garden, trees, and a sky that smells of storm.

But the flamingo is gone.

Just the metal legs remain.

ENTROPIC

31 · Vantage

The hill isn't high, but it's high enough.

From the balcony, I can see the curve of the valley, where the overgrowth has taken back the roads. A year ago – if it's been a year, and time still counts – this would've been a suburb. Now it looks like nature's putting on a show: vines swallowing street signs, driveways furred with moss, trees elbowing their way up through cracked pavement.

I sit with a mug of weak tea cooling in my hands. The ceramic's chipped, but it's warm enough to count. The dog – still just 'Dog' – lies coiled like a question mark at my feet, tail thumping lazily when a fly comes too close. Inside, the house breathes its rituals. Teddy sleeps in, chasing that myth that muscles grow best in REM. Lena's probably in the kitchen by now, coaxing flavour from tins and dusted spice jars.

Me? I prefer the balcony. Always did like the high ground. Rooftops were my thing back in the day – back when 'domain' meant four square blocks of nowhere. Up here, I don't feel tall. Just... less small.

A sound rides the wind. Distant. Could be tin cans rattling, or squirrels brawling in the canopy. I don't flinch. Not unless the dog does. And the dog just went still.

We call the place *The Lookout*, half-joking. It's not a bunker, but it plays one convincingly. Perched right, windows with proper cover, garage you can lock from the inside. Rain behaves. Gutters work. The kind of grace you don't notice until everything else breaks.

From inside, I hear Teddy grunt. Then again. Rhythmic. Could be push-ups. Could be him fiddling with himself. He always counts just loud enough to be heard. Not quite enough to say *come listen*.

I smirk into my tea.

The pantry still blesses us. Beans, not bloated. Rice that doesn't smell like old feet. Bottles with contents you can still name. One tin of peaches. A shrine, basically. No one's said what we're saving it for. We just *are*.

Yesterday, Lena drew birds on the living room wall in charcoal. Not precise, not perfect, but unmistakably birds. She looked skyward as she worked – like her hand was catching echoes of something she used to know.

The water runs hot, most days. Towels dry crisp. Teddy's wearing a belt now. Tucks in his shirt like we're going somewhere. We're not.

Inside, I hear Lena humming again. No song. Just a tone. A resonance. Like her body remembers music better than her mind.

The dog stands, stretches, hops down the steps. Off to nose through the garden again – Teddy calls it that. Really it's two tomato plants, some garlic chives, and a proud row of weeds that catch the light like they're auditioning for a poem.

I lean back. The chair creaks. The breeze brushes my skin like someone exhaling the past.

I close my eyes. Just for a breath.

I could almost believe this is life again.

The dog stops.

No bark. No growl. Just frozen, head tilted toward the treeline. One paw raised like it's forgotten how to finish a step.

I shift in the chair, barely a creak. The mug's gone cold in my hand, forgotten.

There's movement down the slope. Not Gormies. Not deer. Gormies shuffle. They move like they remember being human. Being.

Same ones we've seen before.

They walk like they've got somewhere to be.

Suddenly, they're not at a distance. They're on the road, almost in front of the house. It's unusual.

I set the mug down – quietly. Dog returns to my side without a sound. Doesn't lean, doesn't tremble. Just watches with me.

I stage-whisper to the house. 'Hey.' Just loud enough to reach inside. Not loud enough to carry.

'Quiet. Shhh. Come here.'

They could be friendly, right?

Lena appears at the door a few seconds later. Eyes still soft from whatever she was doing – reading, maybe. Making something. Her gaze follows mine. That, and my nod toward the interlopers.

She doesn't ask. Just steps out barefoot and squints.

Teddy's slower. He wipes sweat off his chest with the hem of his shirt, hair sticking up like he's just hatched. 'We expecting guests?' he mutters.

I jerk my head, sharper than I mean to. Teddy won't take it as an insult – he's too slow to notice. Barely a notch above the Gormies.

Now, he eyes them.

They're closer than ever. Close enough to see the way they carry themselves – arms swinging loose, like civilians. Not shambling on haloperidol like the Gormies.

That's what chills me.

It's not that they're coming.

It's that they belong.

One bends near a shrub, rummages. Finds something – probably nothing – and keeps walking. They're walking past. Two houses down by now.

'Crisis averted,' I say, almost embarrassed to cause such a stir.

Teddy grips the railing like it might leap away. 'Think they saw us?'

'No,' I say, 'but just chill.'

I hold out my hand. *Stop.*

The dog's ears twitch. Something's shifted.

It takes a second to register the sound: a single bark, sharp and high. Too high.

It's the neighbour's mutt – the little one.

We all freeze.

The figures stop too.

Dog answers.

One points. Another shades their eyes. Slowly, inevitably, heads turn toward us.

Not directly. Toward the house.

They start walking again – no rush. Just... this time, on a slightly different angle.

Toward the dog.

Toward us.

I exhale through my nose. Not fear. Not yet. But something clicks into place in my chest. A blueprint for panic drawn up in advance.

Lena whispers, 'We go inside?'

I shake my head. 'Not yet.'

Because there's always a moment – right before the drop – where everything still might turn out fine.

And I want to believe in that moment.

They've clocked us. Locked eyes.

We've got company.

⁂

They're crossing the yard.

No rush. No noise. Just steady steps over the weeds, the gravel, the bones of what used to be a garden path.

I step back inside.

'They're coming,' I say, quiet but firm.

Lena doesn't ask. She's already in motion – slides the kitchen drawer open, pulls a knife, tests the edge with her thumb. Her face is calm, but the way she grips the handle says different.

Teddy bolts up the stairs. Comes back down gripping a cricket bat – notched, weathered, probably ornamental. He holds it like it's heavier than it is. Twirls it once, awkwardly, like he's seen it done on telly. His mouth's open like he's about to say something brave. He doesn't. Probably for the best. He swings like a poet.

'Barricade the door?' Lena asks.

I shake my head. 'Not yet.'

She doesn't push.

We take positions. Not defensive exactly – just... ready. I stand near the front, behind the curtain. Teddy hovers near the stair rail. Lena by the kitchen counter. *Dog* pads between us, tail low but not tucked, ears up, watching everything.

They reach the edge of the yard.

Still no weapons. No shouts.

Just presence.

One stops – tallest of the bunch. Another bends low, extending a hand. *Dog* steps forward. Sniffs. Wags.

No growl. No hackles. Just that easy, dumb trust that animals are either blessed or cursed with.

The tall one looks up.

Eyes find the window. Find me.

And he smiles.

Not wide. Not cocky. Just enough to say: *We see you.*

'I hope we're not interrupting anything,' he says.

His voice is calm. Dusty. Human.

No one breathes.

Lena lowers her knife – a twitch more than a motion.

Teddy sees it. Snaps, 'Don't fall for it. That's how it starts.'

His grip on the bat tightens.

'It's a trope. I've seen it a million times.'

He exhales like he's trying to banish the plot twist.

And for a second – just one second – I let myself believe we might survive this too.

32 · Return to Eden

They have healed the wound of my people lightly, saying, 'Peace, peace,' when there is no peace.

— Jeremiah 6:14

We invite them inside.

Not straight away, of course. There's a ritual to this kind of thing. A careful choreography – step, pause, speak. A slow unwinding of shoulders. Two metres' distance. *Dog*, the diplomat, tail wagging like peace might still be a scent worth chasing.

The tall one offers his name first – Aaron. Thirties, wiry, sunburnt in that seasoned sort of way. He smiles with his mouth but not quite with his eyes. Keeps his hands visible, like he's done this before. Says he's not the leader – just the tallest.

Sure.

Next is Jess. Mid-twenties, hair pulled back like practicality is a habit. Her voice is low, the kind you learn after too many nights whispering over danger. She's the one who asked if we had spare water. That's when I knew they hadn't come to take.

Not yet.

The teen – Milo, I think he says – hangs back. Big kid. Seventeen maybe. Eyes scan like he's playing tactical Tetris with furniture. Doesn't talk much. Keeps close to the girl.

Bea. Ten or eleven. Hoodie swallows her whole. She opens the zip just enough to reveal a second zip inside: a rucksack with a cat tucked in it. Tabby, one eye filmed over like it's watched too many endings. It stares out like it knows what happens to peace.

The last one, Dylan, leans against the porch post like he's waiting for a bus that'll never come. Early twenties, maybe. Quiet, but the kind that isn't shy – just measured. When he speaks, it's to compliment Dog's coat.

Dog approves.

Teddy leans in close. Mutters something caution-shaped.

Probably cribbed from a war movie. Or worse, fancies himself the protagonist.

Lena throws him a look sharp enough to flay. I offer seats. No one sits.

That's smart.

Bea tugs on Aaron's sleeve. He crouches, listens, nods. Turns to us.

'She wants to know if the cat can come inside.'

He says it like it's a serious request. Like it matters.

I glance at *Dog*. *Dog* wags.

Lena smiles. 'If *Dog* doesn't object.'

Dog remains Switzerland.

We eat together.

Canned carrots. Lentils. Powdered what-have-you stirred into warm water. They contribute more than we do, which makes Teddy chew faster. Milo tries out a joke – something about zombie cats. It lands badly enough to draw a laugh.

Bea offers a carrot to the tabby. Tabby blinks slow, like it's not impressed. Then she holds the stare like it's weighing her worth.

I think she's a 'she'.

Later, as the sky fades to ash, Aaron asks if they can camp in the yard.

'Just for tonight,' he says.

Like tomorrow's already promised.

No one says no.

'There's a garden shed out back,' I offer.

It has a door.

That's all they're asking.

Lena gives Bea a candle stub. Bea places it in the rucksack like a relic. The cat shifts closer to the warmth.

And for a few hours – quiet, padded, careful – *Eden almost holds.*

That night, I count new silhouettes against the fence line. Nothing stirs, but I don't sleep. Not fully.

We're learning to hope again. That's always when it gets dangerous.

We gather in the main room, still slightly damp from our respective rinses. The air smells cleaner than usual – steam, soap, faint lemon from whatever Jess added to the rinse bucket. The sun's doing its best to get through the smeared windows, casting a warm blur over the mismatched cushions and folded towels.

Lena starts.

Of course she does.

'Thank you all,' she says, one hand wrapped around a mug, the other resting lightly on the arm of the chair like it belongs there. 'For chipping in. Breakfast, clean-up, all of it. I know it's been… not easy, getting this far. But I'm glad you're here.'

Let's hope it stays this way.

She finishes, 'and I hope the bath and breakfast gave you something close to a reset.'

Bed and breakfast.

She smiles. It's not a big smile. It's the kind that dares people to believe they're safe.

Aaron nods slowly, as if the motion costs something. 'Felt like time travel,' he says. 'Like waking up in a memory.'

Jess doesn't add anything, but the way she exhales tells me she agrees.

Milo chuckles and scratches at a drying cut on his wrist. 'Better than the ditch behind the discount mart. That place had personality, but not plumbing.'

Right.

Bea is curled on the floor with the cat half out of her rucksack. She strokes its side absently, eyes darting between speakers but not speaking herself.

Dylan, as expected, leans back in the chair we'd set out for him like he's assessing the structural integrity of conversation. When he finally speaks, it's to say, 'The light in here feels like a bookshop.'

Not what I expected. Not sure what I expected.

It disarms the room.

Teddy stands near the stairwell, arms crossed, saying nothing. Not hostile, just unmoved. The cricket bat – he still hasn't put it away – rests against the wall beside him like his shadow.

I sip my tea and let the warmth settle. My eyes move from face to face, reading posture, distance, the way people take up space.

Aaron's group is too composed. Not rigid, but fluent – like a crew that's done this before. Settled into other rooms, other kitchens. Which makes me wonder what made them leave those.

Still. They're here. And the room hasn't turned.

Yet.

I pounce on the chance.

'So...'

Not so much 'pounce.'

'We know your names and private backstories, but... Did you know each other before... *this*?'

What is this, exactly?

'We could tell you weren't Gormies—' I wince, too late. 'Anyway, how'd you all meet?'

'You seem like family,' Lena says.

'Not ours,' Teddy adds, drawing ire.

Wanker.

'Jess? Aaron?' I glance at each, in turn.

Bea takes her cat on her lap.

'Not family,' she says. And stops, petting her cat.

Jess takes over.

'Bea and I crossed paths first.'

She looks to Bea and then her pet.

'She already had the cat.'

'And what happened to your family, Bea?' Lena prods.

'Same as the rest.' She rolls her eyes.

Obviously.

'Home long...?' A beat. 'Never mind. So, you and Bea met up with the rest?'

'No,' Bea says. 'Just Milo. Then the rest.'

'And Aaron?' I ask.

Milo answers. 'I found him first.'

'Found *him*?' Aaron interrupts. 'Only pretty sure, I found you...'

Whatever.

'So...' I start to ask something else, change course mid-flight. 'Never mind. Were there others out there like you – like us?'

'You're the first Normies we've run into.' Teddy chimes in. 'Technically, you ran into us.'

I try not to react, but fail.

'Technically, shut the fuck up.'

Teddy – always too clever by half.

'I think we've seen some at a distance,' Aaron says. 'It was tough enough trusting these people. And then you all.'

The room pauses to register the weight of the logic.

''I think we're in a good place,' Lena says.

'Safety in numbers.'

Jess and I say in unison. Then—'Jinx!'

For a moment, the room feels like something we might miss someday.

33 · The Sound

A week later.

Lena wakes me with a whisper and a touch – two fingers on my wrist like a code.

'Hear that?'

So much for a blissful sleep. I do.

Not a bird. Not the wind. Not even Dog, though I can feel him tense by my feet.

The air feels wrong. Not cold, but close. Thick. Charged.

Crash – glass.

The windows.

I bolt up with a start. Reach for the knife under the bedframe.

'Christ, get up!'

She's already upright before I finish the sentence, barefoot, clutching the curtain for a makeshift robe.

The sound of destruction fills the air.

Aaron yells, 'Wake up!'

We're wide awake.

'They're downstairs,' I say, overstating the obvious.

Trousers on. A deep breath. Exhale.

Not ready.

Inhale. I jerk the door open.

Teddy's already at the top of the stairs. Still as stone. Bat in hand.

Lena and I rush to Teddy. Peer over the railing.

It's a fucking siege.

Another figure dashes in and out of view.

'How many?' Lena asks no one in particular but looking at Teddy.

'Can't tell.'

Thuds and screams fill the night.

'We gotta get down there,' I say. 'Gotta help.

'This one's mine,' someone growls. Not a voice I recognise.

It's a bloke.

Silence.

We look at each other.

A muffled struggle gets closer.

'There's more upstairs,' a voice says.

We're upstairs. We've got the position advantage.

'Get ready,' I say, grabbing Teddy's shoulder.

The air smells like fear.

A stranger comes into view at the foot of the stair. Then another – this one holding Jess, covering her mouth with his hand. And another with Bea.

Bea's eyes lock with mine for half a second. Then she disappears behind the man's arm.

Where's the cat?

From nowhere, *Dog* bolts past us, all teeth and fury. Brave bastard. Doesn't make it past the second step.

'Yipe!' One hit. *Dog*'s down. Done for.

'Don't try my patience,' says the one in the front – the one without a hostage. Come on down and make it easier on yourselves. We only want to talk.'

'Fuck you,' Teddy lets out. 'We see how you talk.' He flexes. 'Let's see you come up here.'

A fourth stranger appears. Whispers something to the head man, who turns to look at something out of my line of sight.

'I've got all day, mate,' he says. 'Maybe we'll spend some quality time with the women. Care to join?'

He turns and strokes Jess's face.

She's struggling but going nowhere fast.

'Or are you the type that just likes to watch?'

He takes hold of Bea.

'This one's almost ripe.' He smiles a soulless grin. 'That's okay, though. I'm impatient.' He glares back up. 'Like I said.'

We're helpless and outnumbered.

Lena grabs my hand.

'Do something,' she says.

'Don't worry, love,' he says. 'You'll get your turn.'

'Not gonna happen,' she says, teeth gnashed, knife brandished.

'Don't worry, little lady.'

He glances back.

'Robert here prefers boys.'

Robert grins and nods.

‘The ones down here were too feisty, so they’ve been put down for a long nap.’

He plants a foot on the bottom stair.

‘And now you’ve got a choice – naptime or playtime. Or you can come on down and join the fun.’

Teddy charges down, bat swinging like bravery might make him lighter.

Teddy’s always been thick.

He swings his bat and loses his footing, though he grazes the man’s shoulder.

The intruder throws Bea to the ground and catches Teddy in a chokehold.

‘Run!’ Lena and I shout at Bea at the top of our lungs.

No ‘jinx’ this time.

As quickly as she stands, she’s scooped up by one of the men.

‘Aww…,’ the leader exaggerates. ‘Just you two. You know the score.’

He hands off Teddy to Robert. Picks up his bat off the floor.

‘The fuck is wrong with you?’ I ask.

‘I’ve made you an offer to join us,’ he says, ‘but you don’t seem to appreciate our hospitality. This makes me sad.’

‘Mate, there’s like a million empty houses around here. Why this one?’

‘We ain’t shopping for houses, sweetie. We’re looking for some creature comforts.’

‘Plenty of creatures for comfort out there.’ I point and shrug.

‘Don’t we know it,’ he says. ‘We’re looking to repopulate the earth.’

‘Repopulate with the—’

Not Gormies.

'—those fucking zombies.'

'And maybe we will. But we want some live wires, not some ragdolls.'

Robert starts fondling Teddy.

'We can wait you out,' he says. 'Food's down here. Just you two up there. How long you think you can last?'

I look at Lena and cast my eyes down.

'Fight's down here.'

Fight or flight.

I rush down headlong, knife slicing through the air, then flesh.

My body hits the floor before I feel the pain.

Fading fast, I watch him step over me, casual as dust. The last thing I see is Lena, back pressed to the wall. Still fighting. Still.

34 · Calendar

I hurt myself today
To see if I still feel
I focus on the pain
The only thing that's real
— "Hurt," Nine Inch Nails

Found in a local car park. Author unknown. Undated.

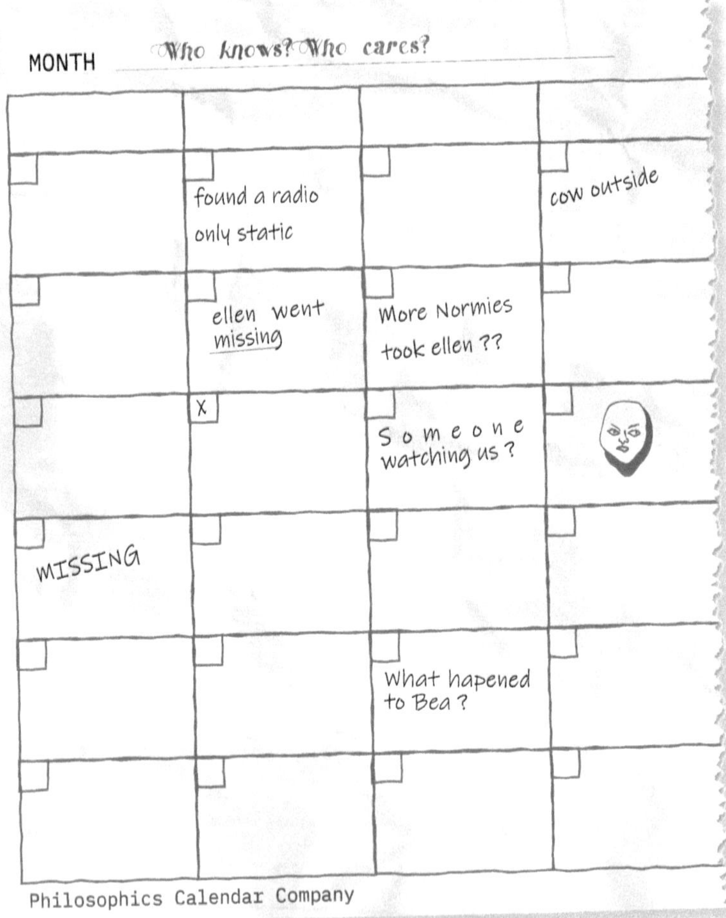
MONTH
Who knows? Who cares?
found a radio
only static
cow outside
ellen went
missing
More Normies
took ellen ??
X
S o m e o n e
watching us ?
MISSING
What hapened
to Bea ?
Philosophics Calendar Company

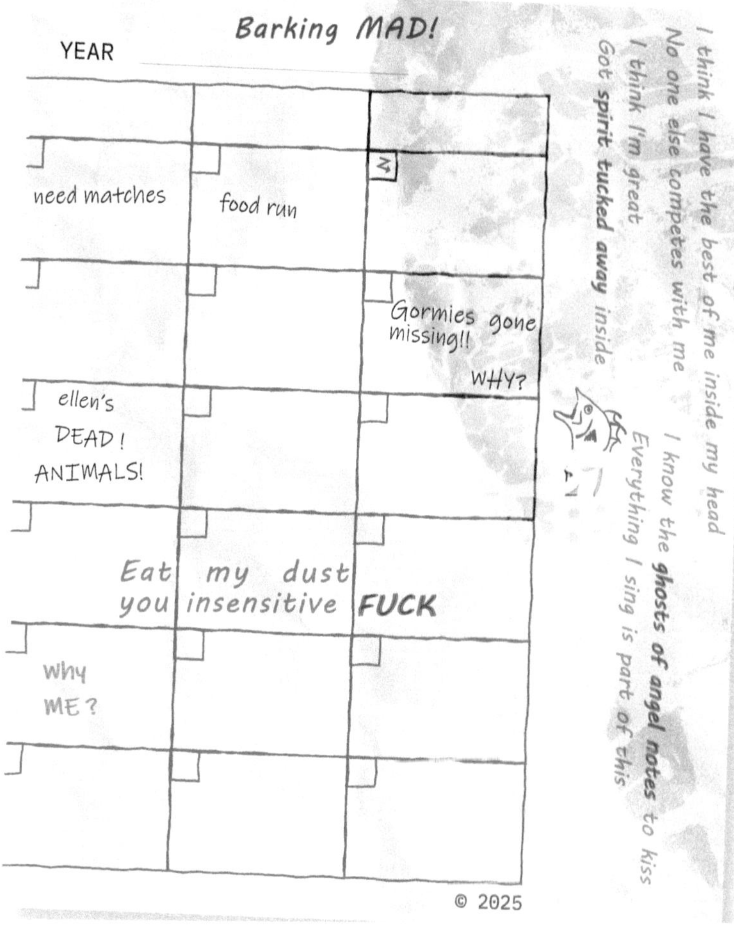

Barking MAD!
YEAR
need matches
food run
Gormies gone missing!!
WHY?
ellen's DEAD! ANIMALS!
Eat my dust you insensitive FUCK
why ME?
© 2025
I think I have the best of me inside my head
No one else competes with me
I think I'm great
Got spirit tucked away inside
I know the ghosts of angel notes to kiss
Everything I sing is part of this

35 · Eunoia

What have I become?
My sweetest friend
Everyone I know
Goes away in the end
— "Hurt," Nine Inch Nails

Time no longer has any meaning – if it ever did.

The earth still rotates, still revolves around the sun, the moon in tow.

Day and night. Rain and shine. Yesterday, today, tomorrow.

But all I can say now is: before, now, and later.

I don't put much faith in later.

Sure, it might get here.

But I'm not sure I will.

But I like living by the sea.

It suits me.

I've been journaling for a while, though I've long since lost track of the days.

Is anyone still keeping track?

And if so – what for?

Time used to feel important, even if only *relatively*.

Now it's just something we used to wear on our wrists.

The sea breeze and the gulls – their cries.

The crash of the ocean on the shoreline.

And the windchimes.

So musical.

Something about ocean air and sunlight gives me energy.

Prana. Qi.

I don't know.

But it invigorates.

It cleanses the soul.

She tends the garden without hurry. No crop schedule. No yield targets. Just rhythm. Hands in soil. A sprout here, a bloom there. Enough to eat. Enough.

The garden affords purpose. Sustenance. *Raison d'être.*

Waves perform their old rites. Gulls shout their gossip into wind. The chimes reply in kind. No audience, yet everything plays its part. All as usual.

Once, the world had dreams of motion. Of acceleration. Progress as escape velocity. But velocity toward what?

She doesn't ask that anymore.

This – this quiet, this morning sun warming his wrist – this is not a fallback. Not ruin. It is *arrival*.

Let the machines rust. Let the computer networks die on their vines. What grows now grows without permission.

No need to rebuild the world. The world is rebuilding *without* us.

She's not lonely. Not precisely. Solitude has shape, and the sea fills it.

Peace was never meant to be built. Only remembered.

Life has returned to normal. Better than *normal* in ways. *Pre-normal*. Progress was always orientated toward a technological future. But that was wrong.

This is progress. Not just *Nature*. Serenity. Peace of mind.

But something is different – felt in the bones, in the soul.

A shadow breaks the water's surface.

Not large. Not loud. Just wrong.

She squints into the horizon, hand raised to the light. Nothing. Just sea, sky, and the line between them.

But something moves.

The wind changes – stranger winds.

The chimes are tangled. Spun too far, too fast. A gust. Or a gale.

Tonight, the wind feels tighter. Coiled. Like breath held too long.

She sleeps with one eye open.

36 · Fragile

She shines in a world full of ugliness
She matters when everything is meaningless
— "The Fragile," Nine Inch Nails

This is you.

Here. Now.

You wake to silence.

Not the kind you trust.

Not the kind that means rest.

The kind that holds its breath.

You reach for the knife, not because you need it, but because you've forgotten how to need anything else.

You curse yourself for not grabbing a gun when you had the chance.

AFO cache.

Stupid.

Probably paranoia.

Then again, you never trusted much.

Not before *this*.

Certainly, not now.

The wind has changed again.

The air smells… wrong. Sour, metallic.

Like breath through teeth.

'Hullo?' you call into nowhere.

You wait.

Count to five.

1

 2

  3

   4

    5

Nothing.

Butterflies. Your stomach knots.

Nerves strung too tight.

Valium would be nice.

Xanax.

Anything, really.

You move to a window.

The garden is still.

The chimes – silent.

No gulls.

No waves.

Just calm.

The wrong kind of calm.

Eerie.

Just you.

Here.

Now.

Probably nothing.

You creep to the door.

Why are you creeping?

Prop it open.

Lean out. Listen.

Nothing.

It is nothing.

Just silence playing dress-up as danger.

You draw the curtains halfway – enough to see, not to be seen.

You put the kettle on.

Not the electric one.

Not anymore. The hob.

Flame, not coil. Gas scavenged. Valves jimmied. Fire.

Like in the old films.

You turn away.

The whistle starts its slow build.

You're not afraid anymore. You're bored of being afraid.

You have three bags of tea left.

Two are herbal.

Chamomile and something called "sleepy breath."

The third is black. Real tea. Strong.

You hesitate.

Black feels too bold for a false alarm. But chamomile feels like surrender.

You go with the black.

No milk anyway. No lemons. that's for sure.

Not out of bravery. Just a mood.

You set the chipped mug on the counter. Pour.

The steam fogs your face.

It smells like a memory of breakfast.

Not any particular breakfast.

Just the idea of breakfast. Nothing particular. Just comfort.

You sip. Burn your tongue a little.

Normal.

You take your tea and step outside.

Not far. Just the stoop. Three concrete steps, moss along the cracks.

Enough to sit and be part of the air.

You inhale.

Salt. Dust. Something vaguely fungal.

The sun's out in that muted way it does now. Cloud-filtered. Tired. But it's light, and light counts.

Across the road, they're back.

Two of them. Gormies.

You watch them like a naturalist.

Not with fear. With curiosity.

You've seen these two before.

One is tall, with a strange tilt to his head, like he's always listening to a sound no one else can hear.

The other smaller, twitchy. Fingernails black. Eyes unfocused.

They walk in slow diagonals. Almost elegant in their nonsense.

You sip your tea.

They stop to examine a shopping trolley turned on its side, touching its wheels like archaeologists.

You imagine David Attenborough narrating this. That soothing voice, explaining madness like it's mating season.

"Here we observe the post-tonal primate in its native habitat – drawn to detritus, seduced by routine."

They don't speak.

They never do.

Have they forgotten or just choose not to?

But they hum, sometimes.

One begins now. A low tone. Nasal. Almost melodic. The other joins in.

It's not music. But it rhymes with something like memory.

You sip again.

The mug warms your hands.

This is peace, you think. Or whatever comes closest.

Then the small one shoves the tall one.

Just a little. Just enough to see if it means something.

The tall one freezes. Turns. Cocks his head.

The small one swings. Once. Twice.

Then it registers: *That's unusual.*

Is the aggressor a Normie?

Why?

The small one turns away. Scans the area. Locks eyes with yours.

Eye contact?

A chill runs up your sternum.

The tall one catches the other with a punch to the face, breaking the lock.

You blink. Hold your breath for a moment.

For fuck's sake.

The other retaliates.

They brawl.

What the—?

The small one lunges low.

The tall one claws at his face.

There's no ceremony. No build-up. Just... escalation.

And when the small one falls, the other rises above him, panting – swinging like a madman. That's when he looks at you again.

Not around.

At you.

You've stopped breathing.

The mug feels suddenly fragile in your hand.

The Gormie tilts his head again.

Not listening.

Tracking.

Not a Gormie.

37 · Escape

I see the dream, and I see the nightmare, and
I believe you can't have the dream without the nightmare.

— Tori Amos

Still you.

Back inside.

Back in the shell.

The curtains are drawn. The door's latched. The windows are braced.

You've done everything right.

But something's wrong.

The house feels smaller than it did this morning.

Smaller than yesterday.

Every room narrowing by a few millimetres.

Two grown ass men hammering on the door.

Your heart pounding harder. Faster.

What happened to the Gormies? Something must have set them off.

That knife. Where is it?

Instinct takes you there. You're armed and dangerous.

You stand facing the door, ready to defend your peace.

You want to pace, but there's no room.

Glass breaks. A bloody hand through the window reaching for the doorknob.

Just reflexes. You lunge and pierce his hand.

He retracts it.

You step back.

His hand again.

Turns the knob.

Too fast to react.

The door's open.

They're inside.

The sanctuary is gone.

You turn and run.

Not far. Not yet.

To the kitchen.

Back door. Bolt. Unbolt. Your hands don't work fast enough.

You hear voices now. Not Gormie moans. Words.

"Get back here so I can kill you," one says.

Doesn't matter which.

"Can't run. Can't hide."

They're laughing.

Like this is a game.

The back door groans. Opens.

You slip through it.

Wood scrapes your hip as you squeeze through the gap.

You sprint.

Across the garden.

Into a neighbour's yard.

You've got some distance.

They've stayed behind.

⁂

You run along the top of the bluff, along the shoreline.

It might be safer down there.

You pause to look.

Just keep running.

Find another house.

Maybe they'll be gone tomorrow. Why are they here anyway? How'd they get so hostile?

Doesn't matter.

Run.

It's far enough away by now. You've got a clear view and a head start.

The air is thick with fear. Waves louder than before.

Sit in the grass and regain composure. Catch your breath.

Take a deep breath.

Hold it.

Hold it.

Exhale.

There's another house. You've passed by it before. Nice view.

Should I even stay near here? I should probably get some distance.

At least you've eaten, but lunchtime isn't that far away.

You go to the house you had in mind.

They probably have something to eat.

You can take it with you.

Inside, you search the pantry for food.

Some cans.

There's a can opener.

All good.

What's that?

Keys. On the counter.

You grab them without thinking.

Momentum takes the rest of you.

Car's in the yard.

Hope the tank's full.

One way to find out.

Turn the key.

Hesitation.

It turns over. It's running.

It's running.

Tank's half full.

Should get some more distance.

Just a little distance.

38 · Panic

So this is where we are
It's not where we had wanted to be
If half the world's gone mad
The other half just don't care, you see
— "World Gone Mad," Bastille

Behind the wheel.

No map. No plan. Just movement.

Forward.

Or, perhaps, just away.

The car hums beneath you. Not confidence—just noise.

The engine stutters when you accelerate too fast, but it holds.

For now.

The house. Long out of sight.

Out of the reach of those things.

You still don't have a word for them.

They're alive.

They're not Gormies.

Not Normies.

Gormies were alive, but not like this. These are people, stripped of limiters.

You pass one walking in the ditch.

He doesn't chase.

Doesn't even look.

Punches a mailbox as you pass.

You keep going.

Radio's useless.

You pass three more crouched around something.

Maybe someone.

One gnaws at a wrist. Another laughs.

The third headbutts a wall until the plaster peels.

You don't stop.

Don't slow down.

Don't scream.

Just drive.

The road narrows. The verge blurs.

Trees blur.

You blur.

You glance in the mirror.

Nothing.

Then something.

Then nothing again.

You breathe again. Shallow at first, then deeper.

Your foot eases off the pedal.

Just for a second.

The road ahead is clear.

Empty.

For the first time in what feels like hours, you let your eyes wander.

There's a blue smudge of sky above the tree line.

Birds, maybe. Or not.

Could be plastic bags.

You don't care.

The wind cuts in through a cracked window.

It's almost clean.

Almost.

You whisper something.

A name, maybe. Or a word. You don't remember.

Just the sound of your own voice, to prove it's still yours.

Ding. Ding.

Amber light flares. Low fuel.

Christ.

A few minutes later.

Ding. Ding.

Christ, my arse. 'Jesus take the wheel,' eh, right?

Another glance to the rearview.

Nothing.

Petrol station ahead.

And so what?

Nothing works. No pumps. No clerks.

All you can do is to keep driving.

Distance is your friend.

Can probably siphon some petrol when I get someplace.

Another glance to the mirror.

Still nothing. No one anyway.

Smack.

You feel the car bump twice, and you jack on the brakes.

What the fuck?

You crack open the door.

Nothing.

You put one foot out and crane your neck to view the area behind the car. You glance back to where the not-Gormies might have been.

Nothing.

You drop to a knee and peer under the car.

A small animal.

What's a dog doing out here? Same as me.

You answer your own question.

Why else?

Not a whimper.

Lucky bastard.

You get back into the vehicle.

Nothing I can do for you, pal.

You drive. Slower this time.

Didn't see the dog.

Another twenty miles.

Wasn't paying attention.

Ding. Ding. Ding. Ding. This time faster.

Really running low.

There's a neighbourhood ahead.

You take a slip ramp into the neighbourhood.

It's the afternoon – from what you remember.

15:10. The clock confirms the time.

If it's right.

Doesn't matter anyway.

Still plenty of daylight.

Any house will do.

You choose the one with the fence in front.

You pull into the drive and turn off the car.

Sit and listen. Roll a window down.

Quiet. A peaceful quiet. Like safety.

If this house doesn't have something to eat, one of the other ones will.

You roll up the window and take your knife – *the* knife.

You won't need it here.

You open the car door and look at the house. It's practically screaming welcome.

Welcome home.

Before you even reach the door, it's over.

The knife falls. Yours no longer.

Theirs now.

39 · Carnage

He who fights with monsters should look to it that
he himself does not become a monster.
— Friedrich Nietzsche

Normies. Gormies.
Gormies, now feral.
Opposites attract.
Like attacks like.

No chance.

No quarter.

No hope.

Every last bastion.
Gnashing. Clashing.
This is no Dr Seuss.

No hats. No cats.
No green eggs or mats.
Just bones in the pantry.
Just screams in the flats.

One fish kills two fish.
Red fish eats blue fish.
The last thing you'll hear is
Knock, knock. "Who's there?"

No Horton. No Whos.
No truffula trees.
Just blood in the soil
and rot on the breeze.

They came with a smile.
They stayed to the end.
You can't count on hope.
You can't phone a friend.

Sneetches and snitches
will leave you in stitches.
No stitches will leave you infected.
Then left for dead.

Unprotected.

40 · Collapse

When we look at a species, we're looking at an experiment.
— Margaret Atwood

Nations, countries, borders, nationality, and races – all retuning to nature.

Humanity 2.0.

But the prospects look bleak.

In the absence of cohesion, things fall apart.

Not metaphorically. Biologically.

What remains of the Normies – small clusters scattered across what used to be nations – hold fast to fading structure.

Routines, rituals, language.

They still whisper to one another.

They still take turns.

They still say please.

Phatic memories intact.

Their survival is fragile, but it is patterned.

And patterns, even when faint, resist erosion.

For a time.

The others – the former Gormies, now something worse – move differently.

The few who still remain call them crack zombies.

No one calls them neighbours.

They do not speak.

They do not group.

They do not remember.

They react.

To movement.

To sound.

To scent.

A crack of glass.

A cough through drywall.

The metallic scrape of a fork.

These are invitations.

They do not strategise.

They do not stalk.

They simply descend.

Without hierarchy or inhibition, they devour.

And without social glue, they turn on each other.

Some claw at their own faces until they reach bone.

Others starve – surrounded by food they do not recognise as edible.

Most die of wounds not inflicted in violence – but left untreated: open sores, infected scratches, wet lungs.

The Normies watch this from behind boarded windows and hastily reinforced doors.

They learn to bury waste again.

To boil water.

To seal wounds.

To whisper.

But they are not alone.

Wildlife creeps back.

The foxes come first, patient and sharp.

Then the dogs – some alone, some in packs.

The air thickens with spores.

The rivers cloud with runoff.

Domesticated fowl revert.

Chickens run feral – leaner, meaner.

Even the insects seem louder now.

What the Normies do not know – what no one has capacity to know – is that their apex has passed.

And apex predators do not climb down the food chain gracefully.

41 · Leviathan

And the life of man, solitary, poore, nasty, brutish, and short.

— Thomas Hobbes

Τηε Ινχομμοδιτεσ Οφ Συχη **A War**

Ωηατσοεϖερ τηερεφορε ισ χονσεθυεντ το α τιμε οφ Ωαρρε, ωηερε **every man is Enemy to every man;** τηε σαμε ισ χονσεθυεντ το τηε τιμε, ωηερειν μεν λιϖε ωιτηουτ οτηερ σεχυριτψ, τηαν ωηατ τηειρ οων στρενγτη, ανδ τηειρ οων ινϖεντιον σηαλλ φυρνιση τηεμ ωιτηαλλ. Ιν συχη χονδιτιον, τηερε ισ νο πλαχε φορ Ινδυστρψ; βεχαυσε τηε φρυιτ τηερεοφ ισ υνχερταιν; ανδ χονσεθυεντλψ **no Culture** οφ τηε Εαρτη; νο Ναϖιγατιον, νορ υσε οφ τηε χομμοδιτιεσ τηατ μαψ βε ιμπορτεδ βψ Σεα; νο χομμοδιουσ Βυιλδινγ; νο Ινστρυμεντσ οφ μοϖινγ, ανδ ρεμοϖινγ συχη τηινγσ ασ ρεθυιρε μυχη φορχε; **no Knowledge** οφ τηε φαχε οφ τηε Εαρτη; **no account of Time; no Arts; no Letters; no Society;** ανδ ωηιχη ισ ωορστ οφ αλλ, χοντινυαλλ φεαρε**, and danger of violent death; And the life of man, solitary, poore, nasty, brutish, and short.**

Ιτ μαψ σεεμ στρανγε το σομε μαν, τηατ ηασ νοτ ωελλ ωειγηεδ τηεσε τηινγσ; τηατ **Nature should** τηυσ δισσοχιατε, ανδ ρενδερ μεν απτ το ινϖαδε, ανδ **destroy one another**: ανδ ηε μαψ τηερεφορε, νοτ τρυστινγ το τηισ Ινφερενχε, μαδε φρομ τηε Πασσιονσ, δεσιρε περηαπσ το ηαϖε τηε σαμε χονφιρμεδ βψ Εξπεριενχε. **Let him** τηερεφορε χονσιδερ ωιτη ημσελφε, ωηεν τακινγ α φουρνεψ, ηε αρμεσ ημσελφε, ανδ σεεκσ το γο ωελλ αχχομπανιεδ; ωηεν γοινγ το **sleep,** ηε λοχκσ ησ δορεσ; ωηεν εϖεν ιν ησ ηουσε ηε λοχκσ ησ χηεστσ; ανδ τηισ ωηεν ηε κνοωσ τηερε βεε Λαωεσ, **and** πυβλικε Οφφιχερσ, αρμεδ, το **revenge all injuries** σηαλλ βεε δονε ημ; ωηατ οπινιον ηε ηασ οφ ησ φελλοω συβφεχτσ, ωηεν ηε ριδεσ αρμεδ; οφ ησ φελλοω Χιτιζενσ, ωηεν ηε λοχκσ ησ δορεσ; ανδ οφ ησ χηιλδρεν, ανδ σερϖαντσ, ωηεν **he locks his chests.** Δοεσ ηε νοτ τηερε ασ μυχη **accuse** μανκινδ βψ ησ αχτιονσ, ασ Ι δο βψ μψ ωορδσ? Βυτ νειτηερ οφ υσ αχχυσε μανσ **nature** ιν ιτ. Τηε Δεσιρεσ, ανδ οτηερ Πασσιονσ οφ μαν, αρε ιν τηεμσελϖεσ **no** Σιν. Νο

more αρε τηε Αχτιονσ, τηατ προχεεδ φρομ τηοσε Πασσιονσ, τιλλ τηεψ κνοω α **Law** τηατ φορβιδσ τηεμ; ωηιχη τιλλ Λαωεσ βε μαδε τηεψ χαννοτ κνοω: νορ χαν ανψ Λαω βε μαδε, τιλλ τηεψ ηαϖε αγρεεδ υπον τηε Περσον τηατ σηαλλ μακε ιτ.

Ιτ μαψ περαδϖεντυρε βε τηουγητ, **there was never** συχη **a** τιμε, νορ χονδιτιον οφ ωαρρε ασ τηισ; ανδ Ι βελιεϖε ιτ ωασ νεϖερ γενεραλλψ σο, οϖερ αλλ τηε **world: but** τηερε αρε μανψ πλαχεσ, ωηερε **they live** σο **now.** Φορ **the *savage* people** ιν μανψ πλαχεσ οφ Αμεριχα, εξχεπτ τηε γοϖερνμεντ οφ σμαλλ Φαμιλιεσ, τηε χονχορδ ωηερεοφ δεπενδετη ον νατυραλλ λυστ, **have no government at all**; ανδ λιϖε ατ **this day** ιν τηατ βρυτιση μαννερ, ασ Ι σαιδ βεφορε. **Howsoever, it may be perceived what manner of life there would be, where there were no common Power to fear**ε; βψ τηε μαννερ οφ λιφε, ωηιχη μεν τηατ ηαϖε φορμερλψ λιϖεδ υνδερ α πεαχεφυλλ γοϖερνμεντ, υσε το δεγενερατε ιντο, ιν α χιϖιλλ Ωαρρε.

Βυτ τηουγη τηερε ηαδ νεϖερ βεεν ανψ τιμε, ωηερειν παρτιχυλαρ μεν ωερε ιν α χονδιτιον οφ ωαρρε ονε αγαινστ ανοτηερ; ψετ **in all times, Kings, and** περσονσ οφ Σοϖεραιγνε αυτηοριτψ, βεχαυσε οφ τηειρ Ινδεπενδενχψ, αρε ιν χοντινυαλλ φεαλουσιεσ, ανδ ιν **the state** ανδ **posture** οφ Γλαδιατορσ; **having their weapons** ποιντινγ, **and their eyes fixed on one another;** τηατ ισ, τηειρ Φορτσ, Γαρρισονσ, ανδ Γυνσ υπον τηε Φροντιερσ οφ τηειρ Κινγδομεσ; ανδ χοντινυαλλ Σπψεσ **upon their neighbours;** ωηιχη ισ α ποστυρε οφ Ωαρ. Βυτ **because they uphold** τηερεβψ, **the** Ινδυστρψ οφ τηειρ Συβφεχτσ; τηερε δοεσ νοτ φολλοω φρομ ιτ, τηατ **misery, which accompanies** τηε Λιβερτψ οφ παρτιχυλαρ **men.**

Ιν Συχη Α Ωαρρε, ***Nothing Is Unjust***

42 · Ashes to Ashes

For dust you are and to dust you will return.

— Genesis 3:19

Vines descend.

Buildings decay.

Creepers climb.

Weeds persist.

Birds Fly.

Petal petal Petal Petal petal Petal

Flower.

Pavement cracks.

43· Unknown

Man starts over again every day, in spite of all he knows, against all he knows.

— Emil Cioran

44 · Vestige

A taxon is Extinct when there is no reasonable doubt that the last individual has died.

— IUCN Red List Definition

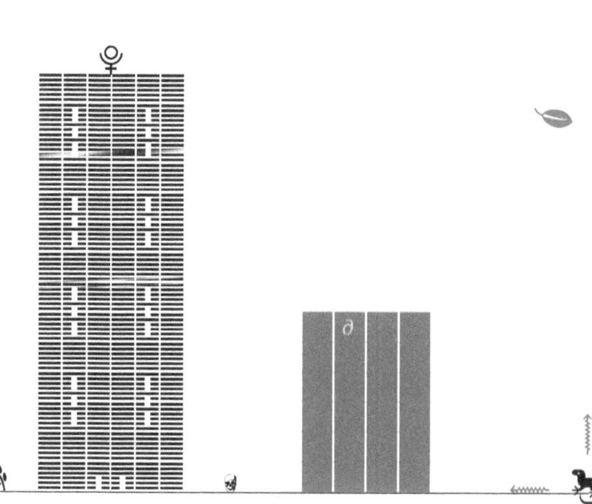

45 · Beatitude

Blessed are the meek, for they shall inherit the earth.
— Mark 5:5

Yet, neither remain

Epilogue

Coming into existence is always a serious harm.
— David Benatar

The gods are gone. Not ascended – erased.

Whatever lingered in the synaptic flickers of belief, in the rituals of a species that mistook noise for meaning, is ash now. The humans carried their gods to extinction. Language followed. Then names. Then memory.

What remains does not speak. It does not worship. It does not ask why.

Some say intelligence might rise again, as if error repeats by necessity. But life is stubborn, not curious. Survival does not require self-awareness. Only appetite.

Ligotti called consciousness a blunder. Benatar called birth a harm. Cioran laughed in despair. Now they rest easier than most. Or rot quieter.

There will be no monuments. No myth. No more gods. Just chlorophyll and bone.

www.ingramcontent.com/pod-product-compliance
Lightning Source LLC
Chambersburg PA
CBHW030545310726
48979CB00010B/2031/J

* 9 7 8 0 9 7 1 0 8 6 9 8 2 *